THE CURSED AMONG US

JOHN DURGIN

PRAISE FOR THE CURSED AMONG US

"Hidden graves, black magic, town legends, and intrepid teenagers - this one has it all, in bloody spades. Durgin's debut manages the impossible: a punchy and gripping horror-thriller sprawled across two decades, crafted with dark obsession and drenched in nostalgia for the golden years of supernatural slasher films." - **Felix Blackwell, author of *Stolen Tongues***

A remarkably malevolent debut that will leave you reaching for your talisman. Durgin takes all the right risks and proves nobody is safe in this impressive coming-of-age novel about a small town with a dark past." - **Joshua Marsella, author of *Hunger For Death***

"The Cursed Among Us is a horror novel with its heart in the right place—ready to be ripped out! Containing surprising and sometimes stunning emotional depth, this homage to '90s B-movies and supernatural documentaries explores the agony of growing up and holding onto friendships when the world seems determined to rip everything you love apart." - **Joseph Sale, author *Dark Hilarity***

"The Cursed Among Us is a coming-of-age, small town horror blast, one that I think a lot of people will really enjoy." - **Steve Stred, Splatterpunk-Nominated author of *Sacrament* and *Mastadon***

THE CURSED AMONG US

Copyright © John Durgin 2022

John Durgin has asserted his right under the Copyright, Designs and Patents Act 1988 to be identified as the author of this work.

This book is a work of fiction and, except in the case of historical fact, any resemblance to actual persons, living or dead, is purely coincidental.

ISBN: 9798426361584

This book is sold subject to the condition that it shall not, by way of trade or otherwise, be lent, resold, hired out, or otherwise circulated electronically or made free to view online without the publisher's prior consent in any form of binding cover other than that in which it is published, and without a similar condition, including this condition, being imposed on the subsequent purchaser.

Cover Art by Matt Seff Barnes

Interior Formatting by Joshua Marsella

For Danielle, Will, and Elizabeth. May our family remain protected from the curse...

"There's little good in sedentary small towns. Mostly indifference spiced with an occasional vapid evil—or worse, a conscious one."

Stephen King | Salem's Lot

PROLOGUE
1980

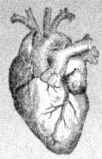

HENRY BLACK TREKKED THROUGH THE DENSE FOREST AS DAWN approached, dragging the girl's body behind him. The distinct aroma of fetid earth hit his nostrils while he searched the area to make sure nobody had followed him. He squinted as the morning sun poked up over the horizon, the light coming through the treetops, decorating the ground with polka-dots, lighting dead tree trunks and fallen branches. He'd tied the body at the hands and feet with a thick rope, as he had with all the others. He needed to hurry—there was no telling how long she would remain unconscious. Earlier, Henry had used a rock and cracked it over the back of her head to knock her out. Even though she only weighed north of a hundred pounds, his arms and legs were starting to get tired trying to pull her across the rough terrain. Considering how many times he'd done this over the past few months, he would have thought he'd built up some endurance. In his defense, he left the other bodies much closer to the trails, not caring if someone discovered them. This one, however, he never wanted to be found. *She*

was the reason this all started, and now it was all going to come to an end.

It was still dark out when Henry arrived at the cemetery, making it easy to remain hidden while he pulled the body out of his trunk and entered the woods. He still couldn't shake the feeling of being watched. It must have been a few miles out at this point, a place nobody would ever search. Curled, brown leaves covered the ground, absent of any small prints of wild rodents or birds. He'd hiked far enough off the path; it was time to look for a burial site.

The forest cleared up ahead, an open field for the day's early light to shine down upon. Beyond the field, the forest seemed like a wall of darkness, the perfect spot to hide a body. Whatever it took to stop the voice in his head. For months, she had infested his mind, telling him what to do. Who to *kill*—controlling him like a sadistic puppet-master.

Even with the cool spring morning air, sweat dribbled down his forehead as he pushed on. When he got to the copse of trees, he dropped her legs, and left the body behind to scout the area. Henry tossed his bag to the side and ducked down, crawling under a fallen tree hiding behind some underbrush. The sharp, rigid bark on the bottom of the tree scraped along the back of his shirt, sending a jolt of pain across the surface of his skin. Cringing, he got up on the other side and scanned the area. This was it, the spot where he would end this nightmare.

Picking up the backpack, he unzipped it and pulled out the miniature shovel he'd packed. Digging a hole big enough for a body with such a small tool would be difficult, but determination drove him to do what he had to do. For now, the voice remained silent. It was the first time he recalled having his own thoughts in weeks. A quick glance back at the body still lying motionless brought some relief, but he feared she would likely wake any minute. Not that she could do anything about it—he'd tied the rope tightly and gone through extra measures to make sure she could not escape. He just worried about the voice coming back, a vibration in his head like someone slamming rocks against the inside of his cranium.

The hole came along much quicker than he expected. Somehow, he'd found a spot free of any excessive tree roots with mostly soft soil to dig up. In a perfect world, he would have preferred to dig deeper, but he was up against time, and this would have to do. Henry wiped the sweat from his face and threw the shovel aside. Birds twittered, flying from tree to tree overhead, as if watching their daily sitcom below. He double-checked his bag to confirm he'd brought everything else he needed, and then hopped the fallen tree, ready to drag the body to the hole. She still lay motionless, looking beautiful in the pink hues of the morning light. Her long, black hair blew in the light breeze, giving her the appearance of being at peace. Part of him wanted to kiss her, and those perfect, alluring lips, one last time. But that would be a grave mistake, likely leading to him second guessing what he planned to do and the whole plan unraveling before his eyes. Gritting his teeth, he grabbed her legs and marched toward the hole. When he got to the fallen tree, he hopped it and pulled her body underneath. Again, he let go of the legs and took a few deep breaths.

"I'm sorry it had to be this way... It's the only way I can know for sure nobody else gets hurt... I love you," he said to the unconscious body.

With one last look at her, he rolled her into the hole. The body turned over and landed on its back, the face staring up with her eyes remaining shut. Henry picked up the shovel and prepared to fill the hole. When he glanced back down, her eyes bulged open wide, glaring back at him with a crazed stare. She screamed, sending chills down his spine. Henry slammed the shovel down into her face, leaving a gash from her forehead down to her chin. Blood trickled down her cheek as her eyes fluttered in and out of consciousness again. He quickly covered the body with the moist dirt, hiding the face so he did not have to look at her anymore. He went as fast as his hands let him operate, exerting all his energy. When he'd finished, he took out the other supplies from the bag and set them up around the burial site.

For a few moments he stood, crying over her grave. They were tears of sadness, but also tears of relief. Relief of knowing this was all over now, that the voice inside his head would be gone forever and the town would be protected. He took a bunch of loose branches from the surrounding area and carefully laid them over the top of her grave to be sure it would remain hidden to the naked eye. Henry Black picked up his bag, put the shovel inside, and zipped it up. He looked down at the newly filled hole, staring at the spot he'd just buried his wife, and headed back out of the forest.

CHAPTER ONE
1999

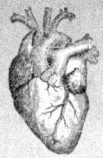

HOWIE BURKE WOULD HAVE LOVED TO ADMIRE THE VIBRANT autumn forest, perhaps lying on his back, staring up at the leaves while they danced to an unheard beat. He would have loved to enjoy the silent dusk creeping in on the warm fall night. It all would have been far more pleasant if not for the masked killer walking toward him.

Fear spread across Howie's face, his lips quivering as the figure approached. He backed up on all fours in a crab walk position, trying to maintain the distance between them. Howie did not dare trying to stand and make a run for it, afraid to take his eyes off his massive enemy. The killer's mask was white, with emotionless facial features, red paint dripping down from the eyes like tears of blood. A torn flannel shirt that looked like it'd survived the world's worst car wreck—spattered in blood, dirt, and God knows what else—covered lacerations across the killer's chest. In his hand, he held a long machete he squeezed with an iron tight grip. Matching blood dripped down the blade, making it some demented accessory to his outfit.

The figure continued his slow and steady stride toward

Howie. Vivid oranges blanketed the forest floor, a soft crunch emitting with each step of the pursuer's boots. He got closer and closer, and Howie froze in place, staring up at the monster. Looking up from his worm's eye view, he watched the killer raise the machete high above his head—the day's last bit of sun gleaming off the blade. A drop of blood dripped from the metal, landing right in Howie's eye.

"Oh, what the hell man, come on!" Howie yelled.

"Cut! *Cut!*" a voice came from the side.

Howie glanced over toward the woods and saw his friends walking toward him. His best friend, Cory Stevens, held a video camera at his side and appeared extremely annoyed. A rolled-up script stuck out of his back pocket. Next to Cory stood Ryan Star—all two hundred and fifty pounds of him. Ryan wore coke-bottle glasses a few inches thick, his eyes magnified behind the lenses giving him a constant look of surprise. He wore his customary camouflage army pants and work boots. A bag of props hung over his shoulder. The weight of the bag had taken its toll on Ryan while they climbed up the incline to the scene's location.

Howie's eye stung as he tried to blink the pain away.

"What's in that stuff? This burns so bad!"

The killer took off his mask, revealing the face of Todd Seymour—the clown in their band of misfits. His default face consisted of a squinting set of eyes that Gilbert Gottfried would be proud of, curly brown hair resting on top of his large dome of a head. Todd laughed like someone had told the world's best joke. He looked at Howie and flicked the end of the machete down, sending more blood into Howie's face, letting out another roar of laughter.

"Guys, come on, stop acting like children. The daylight's almost gone, and we only have a few more scenes to try and finish out here tonight before it gets too dark," Cory said.

He pulled the script out of his back pocket and studied it over, flipping through the pages, and stopped—once again looking frustrated. Cory carried a skinny build, even by ninth grade standards. His pale skin feared light enough that even the thought of the sun brought on the sensation of burning. He blew his long bangs out of his eyes so he could focus on the pages in his hand.

"Shit! We forgot to shoot the scene with the Killer chasing Howie through the forest that leads up to this moment. God damn it." Cory gazed up at the sun, now sinking down beneath the trees. "Okay, here's what we need to do. Forget this scene, we need to go further into the woods to film the chase scene first. The light will be worse in there, and we need to film what we can before it's too late. We can come back to this scene tomorrow when we shoot."

Todd stared down at Howie and let out a snarky laugh. He started to walk towards the forest and said, "Plus, we know Howie has to be home in time to be tucked in for bed. What fifteen-year-old has a curfew anyway?"

Howie stood up, dusting off his clothes, continuing to squint in pain from the fake blood. It always frustrated him that of all his friends, he remained the only one forced to be home early. Sure, they were only fifteen years old, but it's not like they got into trouble. Hell, they'd never even touched alcohol let alone done any drugs. Filming a horror movie in the woods behind the cemetery was their big weekend adventure. His mom insisted, however. She said she understood that they were good kids and wouldn't find themselves in any trouble. She told him it was more of a safety issue. He needed to promise his parents every time he went out with the guys that they would never go too far out into the woods. Specifically, *these* woods. They remained very adamant about this request, and his dad was not one to be disobeyed. Far too often, Howie would do something that most parents would consider minor—kids being kids —but that his dad would consider a much more consequential act of defiance. From an early age, his dad had talked in a loud, stern voice, threatening Howie if he ever went against the rules. He was a towering man, built in a way that his true strength didn't show on the surface, but the term "country strong" fit him. After years of working in the woods, his dad had filled out with a stocky build and callused hands that shouted "rough around the edges" to anyone who shook them. As Howie got older, his dad's firm tone transitioned to something much worse. His dad insisted he no longer intimidated his son by only raising his voice, so he started raising his hands instead. Howie learned firsthand how callused those palms really were anytime he so much as blinked at his dad the wrong way. For the most part, Howie had learned when to avoid his dad's short temper. When to hide out in his room and read his comics, or his horror novels, and escape from reality. Sometimes, Howie had trouble keeping his revulsion for his dad buried inside—even though he knew what would happen if he spoke up.

Logic was hard to uncover with many of the rules Howie had to follow. For one, his dad let him watch any horror movie he wanted, all the sex and gore included. Yet, he blocked MTV because he said it was inappropriate for a kid. So, like any teen would naturally do, Howie questioned the decision. It seemed reasonable to try and talk about it. Why could he enjoy someone's head being cut off, yet he couldn't fantasize about Britney Spears dancing around in a schoolgirl outfit? His dad didn't feel like being questioned that day, and instead, almost broke Howie's arm while dragging him to his room and forcing him to watch while he shattered a good deal of Howie's horror movie VHS collection to pieces. Instead of seeing Howie's point of view and easing up on the music video restrictions, he doubled down and told him no more horror movies. Luckily, like many of the stupid rules in place, his dad forgot about it over time.

Many similar examples played through Howie's mind every time he thought of upsetting his dad. His mom was more understanding, but she was also intimidated by her husband's anger and usually kept quiet anytime the scolding began. Howie learned to live with this on a daily basis, but it didn't mean he planned to intentionally go out of his way to do something his dad would flip his lid over. Curfew happened to be one of those hard lines he would never cross.

He'd given up trying to figure out his dad long ago. In his entire fifteen years of living, he didn't recall ever seeing his dad take a sip of alcohol. So, he wasn't that proverbial angry drunk who took it out on his family. No, it was much more complicated than that. A fire burned deep inside his dad, and everyone around him had to avoid getting burned by it.

The group continued to walk deeper into the woods, the light fading with each step behind the shelter of extended tree-limbs. Over the last few years, they had filmed many movies—mostly rip-offs of other horror movies they loved—but they had never been this far into the forest. Gnarled roots dipped in and out of the ground, making each step a burden. Evidently, nobody else had ever gone out this far neither. Any sign of a path was long gone, the trail snaking through the undergrowth. Branches decorated the forest floor. To say they had ventured off the beaten path was an understatement. There was no way they'd make it back to the entrance of the Cemetery before nightfall. Howie dreaded going home to face punishment, likely grounded—

or worse—which was the last thing he wanted a week from Halloween. He and the guys lived for this time of year—giving that up would be a crushing blow to him and his friends. Howie stopped walking and glimpsed over at them.

"Okay, this has to be far enough, right? You only need a shot of the Killer chasing me through the woods, and me tripping over something? Why are we going out so damn far?" Howie asked.

"This is fine, I guess. If we wait too much longer the camera won't pick up the shot anyways. I should've brought the stupid lights with me," Cory said.

Ryan set down the bag of props, sweat stains forming in his armpits. His glasses began fogging up from his forced, heavy breathing.

"I didn't sign up for a fucking hike, this is killing me."

Todd laughed and pointed at Ryan's face. "Oh my god, look at his glasses! You need windshield wipers on those things, fat ass."

Ryan walked toward Todd aggressively, ready for a fight but Todd backed off and held up his hands.

"Man, take a chill pill. A fat kid being forced to walk miles in the woods against his will. All the camouflage in the world couldn't hide that joke," Todd said, while fleeing from Ryan's reach.

"For Christ's sake Todd, grow up. Can you focus for two minutes, so we can get this done please? I don't really have the desire to end up on another episode of Unsolved Mysteries," Cory snapped.

"Gosh, sorry Debbie downer," Todd muttered under his breath.

An episode of Unsolved Mysteries had focused on the town of Newport. Just over twenty years ago, a serial killer had terrorized their town. A string of gruesome murders had sent Newport into a panic. Howie's parents would not tell him all the details, but that is why the library existed. Along with getting hooked on horror novels, Howie took the time to visit the newspaper archive that the school library stored away. He was fascinated by the whole story and read every little detail—at least every detail released to the public.

The victims had all been found with their chest torn open. The reports said the bodies appeared to be ripped apart with hands, something that sent the town into a frenzy. Claw marks were visible on each of the bodies where they got pulled apart—their hearts had all been removed from the chest. With the first body, police assumed an animal must have done it. It was far too vicious for anything else. That was the initial thought. When they moved the body from the snow and put it into a body bag, the cops on the scene discovered raw, irritated skin on the wrists and ankles. It showed signs of a body that had been tied up and dragged. After that discovery, it turned into a murder investigation. Over the next few months, bodies started to show up in the surrounding woods, murdered in the same fashion. Every single one of them had been transported deep in the forest, chest torn open, heart ripped out. The rope lacerations marked each set of limbs.

Howie had been lucky enough to score a copy of the Unsolved Mysteries episode from their friend Lucas, who worked at the movie store in town. The VHS had been worn out a bit—it had been filmed in the eighties and viewed many times over the last fifteen years. Howie and his friends rented it over and over, trying to find possible inspiration for the horror movies they made. The episode focused on the killer's wife and how her body had never turned up. The killer, named Henry Black, refused to tell any of the authorities the location of her body, saying the world remained a better place without her.

While Howie understood the reasons these woods were deemed off limits, he didn't understand why it was such a big deal *now*. The killer had been captured, put in jail, and as he discovered in one of the old newspapers, the guy died years ago in prison. So, why all the fuss?

Gesturing towards the woods, Cory attempted to get Todd moving.

"Don't take it so seriously, it's not like you're paying us to film this thing. I only agreed so I could pretend to kill all of you—and so I'd be able to touch Bethany without you getting pissed at me," Todd said.

Cory shook his head disgusted. Bethany was Cory's crush and playing the lead role of the film. Todd would hold her down in the final battle of the movie before she would eventually kill him, surviving as the final girl.

"The closest thing to reality in that scene might be that she *actually* kills you, damn pervert. Now shut up and put the mask back on. We need to do this in one take," Cory said.

Todd pulled the mask over his face and snagged the machete from the prop bag, holding it between his legs and said, "Come to Daddy, Howie!"

Howie rolled his eyes and started to walk towards the clearing. He stretched his legs a bit, knowing he needed to run as fast as possible in the scene. Cory clapped his hands together to catch everyone's attention, and they all looked in his direction. For a fifteen-year-old kid, Cory took the craft very personally. Howie respected how focused Cory got while making these films. It was his true passion—in his mind he wanted to make the next blockbuster movie. The others in their group sometimes found themselves frustrated with how urgent he treated the whole experience. They saw it as screwing around and having fun, but to Cory, this was a job.

Howie and Cory had been best friends since third grade. They had both been playing alone with their ninja turtle action figures at recess when they spotted each other and started comparing collections, and the rest was history. Their relationship grew closer over the years and the two of them became inseparable after an awful night when Cory slept over and witnessed Howie's dad hurting him. Howie begged Cory not to say anything and pretend he never saw it. As much as he suffered at home, he loved his parents and the last thing he wanted was to be forced into foster care and move away from his friends. Besides, he'd heard horror stories of kids who got adopted and put into far worse situations than the one they had come from. Kids being locked in basements and being fed scraps from the table for dinner. Kids being more than physically abused. He had it rough, but at least he understood what he had and could escape it when he hung out with his friends. Cory had been as loyal as any best friend could be, and Howie was thankful they shared such a close friendship.

"Okay, let's do this. Howie, you know the drill. When I say action, run as fast as you can until you hit the thicker area of trees up there. Todd, please try not to fuck this up again. We have one shot at this before it's too dark," Cory said.

Cory held up his hand as Howie and Todd waited for their sign. When he yelled action, Howie raced toward the mouth of the forest. Todd followed him in the standard slasher movie brisk walk. The white mask they had picked for the movie really did kind of creep Howie out as he peered back over his shoulder giving his best frightened reaction for the camera. After reading up on how the *Halloween* mask had been made, they wanted to do something similar in hopes to create the next iconic slasher movie. The mask had been spray-painted white; the eyes painted a dark red with blood dripping down the cheeks.

Howie ran as fast as he could, hopping over rotten trees and ducking under bushes. Now in the thicket of the forest, branches whipped him in the face with each step. Bracing himself for the planned fall, he intentionally stumbled over his own foot and came slamming down on his stomach. The wind rushed out of him, and he gasped to catch his breath. He heard the heavy feet of Todd crunching on the dead leaves prowling behind. Cory yelled cut and the scene came to an end—they had nailed it on the first take, a rarity for them. Howie rolled over to his back, holding his stomach in agony.

As he waited for the others to come closer, he spotted something odd over in the tall grass to his left. He got to his feet and walked over for a closer look. To anyone unfamiliar with this deep part of the woods, it would most likely appear as just some fallen tree limbs. But as Howie got closer, he realized the branches and twigs had been laid out with the intention of hiding something. He crouched for a better view. Something deep inside him said to avoid touching the branches—looking at them gave him the chills. Why had it never been discovered? Sure, nobody wandered this far out, but there had to have been a stray jogger who went for a run through the forest? Or a party that the seniors threw in a secret location to hide from the cops? Underneath the branches, he could make out something shiny and black. It appeared to be a stone, with a strange design painted on its surface. *So weird*, he thought. He was so focused on the symbol that he did not hear his friends coming up behind him.

Todd reached out and squeezed Howie's shoulder, still in character. Howie jumped, letting out a small yelp. The quiet forest erupted with laughter, and he could feel his face warm with embarrassment.

"Real funny, assholes. You might not laugh as much if you come over here and see this. What is this thing?" Howie asked.

They all glanced at the strange geometry that had been drawn on the rock. It was impossible to get a good view with it mostly covered up. Ryan knelt, squinting through his glasses.

"I don't know what it is, but I sure as hell won't be touching it. Looks like some kinda creepy grave or something. Is that black glass?" Ryan asked.

Cory walked up and put the camera to his face, hitting record.

"No, it looks like a rock of some kind. Well, this will make for a fun moment in the making-of-video. I dare one of you to touch it for the camera."

Todd pulled the mask up, then pushed past them and scoffed. If anyone was going to do it, it was him. He leaned over and inched his hand closer. When his hand contacted the first branch, he started shaking uncontrollably, his eyes began rolling into the back of his head. At first, everyone started laughing at him assuming he was joking. The convulsions intensified, Todd dropping to his knees. Cory set the camera down on the ground, Ryan and Howie grabbed hold of Todd and tried to snap him out of it.

"Come on man, stop messing with us," Ryan said uncertain.

Howie prepared to slap Todd, desperate to snap him out of his trance when suddenly Todd stopped, his face zoned in on the ground. He stood for a moment frozen in place. A deep laugh forced itself out of him, and he peeked up at them unable to hold the smile back anymore. They should have known; it was typical of Todd to mess with them. Early on in their childhood he had been quiet and reserved—kept to himself. When sixth grade came along, he was like a new kid. Howie remembered the first time he saw the change in English class. Ms. Renfroe had asked the class if they knew anything about the similarities of sonnet and concrete poems. Todd raised his hand to say that he did in fact know a similarity of the two styles—they both were boring as hell. This got some laughs out of the classroom, but it also got Todd detention and sent to the principal's office. His parents were not thrilled, but Todd loved every second of the attention. He was no longer in the background, ignored by all the cool kids. It was like a switch had been flipped, and at that moment, he'd deemed the class comedian well suited him.

Ryan pushed Todd to the ground, knocking him on top of the pile of sticks. The branches scattered, displaying not one black stone but many spread out around a mound of dirt that was overgrown with weeds. The laughter on Todd's face swiftly changed to a mix of anger and fear. He glanced down and found his fingers firmly penetrating the soil up to his knuckles. A sharp prick shot up through his hand and he jumped off the pile of branches, erratically wiping his hands on his clothes like he had fallen on a mound of poisonous spiders.

"Why the hell did you do that, Ryan?" Todd asked.

Tension filled the air. Filming all day was grueling enough, and the uneasy sense coming over them only added to the stress.

Ryan looked down in shame, embarrassed he had let Todd under his skin. "I'm sorry man, you just haven't stopped all day with this stuff and it's exhausting. Let's go home and forget about it, okay?"

"Forget about it? Everything is exhausting to you fatty. I'm so sick of you getting so butt hurt over every damn joke.

We all pick on each other, yet you act like some sad victim. Get over it!" Todd shouted.

Ryan was about to respond when they heard the snap of a branch in the distance. It was too dark in the crowded woods to see anything; the sun had long ago dropped below the top of the pines. They froze in place, listening for any other sounds of an approaching animal or person—and heard nothing at all. The sounds of the forest were strangely absent. No birds chirped; no squirrels jumped from tree to tree. They were alone.

Another branch broke—much closer this time. Without thinking, they all ran in the direction they had come from. Cory snatched up the camera. Ryan picked up the supply bag. Todd and Howie trailed behind them, both looking back toward the trees. Sunset had finally drained out of the sky overhead, leaving the woods in shadow. It made it hard to make anything out, but Howie was certain he spotted the outline of a figure watching them. He kicked into high gear, trying to dodge overhanging branches—his heart pounding in his chest as the damp fall leaves slid across his face like wet tongues. Still focused on the scene behind him, he slammed right into the back of Cory, sending the camera flying out of his hand and smacking off the ground. Cory dropped to the ground and picked up the camera, clutching it to his chest like he had dropped a baby on its head.

"No, no, no. What'd you do Howie!" Cory exclaimed. He was looking at the device closely, inspecting it for any damage.

Howie was oblivious to what he had done to the camera. Unable to take his focus from the tree-line, he was convinced something peered back at them. But all he saw was empty darkness—any sign of the silhouette was gone.

"Did you guys not see something back there?" Howie asked.

"I don't care about some stupid fucking animal looking at us. News flash—the forest is full of animals, Howie!" Cory said.

Still looking back, Howie shook his head. "I know what I saw man, that was no animal. We need to get the hell out of here like right now."

Cory slid his hand back and forth over the screen, revealing a small crack. He shut it slowly and stuck it in the camera case with a big sigh. Looking at Howie he said, "It doesn't appear to be broken, but my parents are going to kill me once they see the crack in the screen dude. What am I supposed to tell them? We aren't allowed out here —*remember*?"

Howie felt terrible. Cory was his closest friend, and he'd just busted his prized possession. He knew that if any of the others broke it, things would be far worse. It didn't help the guilt he felt.

"I'm really sorry. I can talk to my parents about giving some money to help fix it or get a new one. I—" Howie's sentence was cut short by a menacing screech coming from the darkness. The noise got louder, forcing them to cover their ears. The wind intensified as the volume increased, tree limbs thrashed and snapped in every direction. Almost in unison, they screamed in terror. They did not wait around to get another glimpse. Only moments ago, Howie was running from a fake murdering psychopath. Now he felt his life was really in danger. He had never seen Ryan run so fast—all of them ran faster than ever before in their lives. They continued their sprint through the forest, trying to head in the direction they thought would bring them to the entrance. The woodland was getting so dark everything started to look the same, making it a guessing game as to which direction to head. Some of the landmarks looked familiar, but panic fueled them to continue forward without pausing to get their bearings. The trail gradually became more visible, a sign that they were headed the right way. Up ahead, the back of the cemetery appeared around the corner. As the day's last light faded away, they made it back to their bikes hidden behind the cemetery shed.

"What... the hell... was that?" Todd forced out between deep breaths.

Cory made sure the camera bag was zipped up and secure and hopped onto his bike. "I don't know, but I won't be hanging out to see if it comes any closer."

CHAPTER TWO

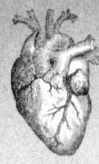

THE TOWN OF NEWPORT, NEW HAMPSHIRE HID IN THE SHADOWS of larger surrounding towns. With a population of just over six thousand people, pretty much everybody knew each other. Newport consisted of three schools, which for such a small population seemed a bit excessive. One for elementary, middle school, and high school. It was a town that prided itself in the success of its sports program. The football team wore their orange and black jerseys to school every Friday during the season, with chants of "go Tigers" and "go get em this weekend" ringing down the hallway every time they made their journey to their next class. Some would say sports took precedence over education, with athletes often coasting through classes to grades they had no business achieving. Politics in a small town were nothing new, but Newport wore that statement on its sleeve, not afraid to promote the football team over education. There remained a power hierarchy in town that had been in place since the sixties, and it appeared to be going nowhere anytime soon.

The town wasn't all bad though—there remained a

tight knit community that would do anything to support one another. A town where your neighbor was also your teacher, restaurant owner, or mechanic. As far as entertainment went, there was a bowling alley where teens met on the weekend to bowl and play pool, a video store that somehow maintained a loyal customer base with Blockbuster opening one town over, and a rec center with a basketball court, weight room, and indoor pool. That was it. For a town where family incomes were below the national average, many people found it difficult to afford more. The big event for high-schoolers was doing the "McDonald's 500", which consisted of a drive from the high school parking lot on the north end of town through downtown, where all the local shops and restaurants were located—including McDonald's—where they would drive around the drive-thru without ordering anything and head back to the school parking lot. This was done to see if anyone they knew was out and about. That, and it was an excuse for them to blast their music with the windows down so everyone could hear them listening to the newest DMX, Jay-Z, Korn, and even Garth Brooks albums.

It was a town where one barbershop existed. Every dad brought their son as a rite of passage to Spunky's Barbershop. Spunky would yank on kid's ears and tell the kids he was stretching them out to make them fly like Dumbo while the dads all talked town gossip and sports.

Two pizza shops, a breakfast place, and a sub shop in the back of a convenience store provided locals with a little variety for a night out. A campground sat at each end of town, attracting many tourists in the summer who wanted to escape from the everyday grind. It was a boring life, but one that most of the residents strove to maintain. The police station consisted of only five officers, led by the heavyset Joshua Miller, who had been on the force since he graduated from college. He had a lot of pull in the town, and many of the townsfolk feared him, knowing he could make their life a living hell if he wanted to.

A train track sat around the perimeter of town, used mainly to deliver parts to the two factories that a high percentage of the residents worked at, often for years on end. There was a gun factory, where some of the country's top guns were built, and there was a wool factory. A normal day in the life of the town's working class consisted of an eight-to-ten-hour shift at one of the factories, heading down to the bowling alley to toss down a few drinks with the crew, and heading home to eat dinner before watching the nightly sitcoms. Rinse and repeat every day of the week.

The main cemetery was off a side road in town, much larger than the population would dictate. Surrounding the cemetery were acres upon acres of forest, and outside of the first few miles, the area had been left alone, nature long ago taking over and never letting go. This also happened to be the area that most of the town deemed off-limits. After the murders years ago, many rumors spread around town as to what went on out there, but they all agreed on one thing in the town meetings—stay out. Everyone had their own reasons, but it was a universal decision. Officer Miller even implemented significant fines for anyone discovered out there.

The way Howie and his friends saw it, rules were meant to be broken. Now they were seeing firsthand why those rules had been put into effect.

CHAPTER THREE

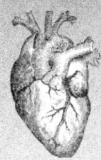

Howie parked his bike in the garage and glanced at his watch. Somehow, he'd managed to arrive home only ten minutes after curfew. Hopefully his dad would take it easy on him since he was only a few minutes late.

He could hear the television through the wall of the garage, likely one of the boring westerns his dad sat through every night. Any hope his dad would not be waiting in the living room for him to get home vanished. Taking a deep breath, Howie walked inside. As expected, his dad sat in his worn-down recliner with the remote resting on his stomach. A black and white movie played on the screen; a cowboy was in the middle of shooting a group of thieves outside of a saloon. His dad shifted his attention from the television; the expression on his face could have fooled the world's best poker player. Howie had no idea what to expect, his dad didn't look mad, but he sure as heck wasn't smiling either.

"Do you know how to tell time, Howie?"

"Yes... Dad. I'm really sorry I'm late. We got stuck talking to Mr. Carl in town, I kept telling him we had to go home before I was late for curfew," Howie said, lying through his teeth.

He had thought of the excuse on the way home, hoping that if his dad thought he was talking to a teacher that he would at least take it a little easier on him. It was obvious his dad was not pleased with the excuse. Howie could see his jaw tightening as he ground his teeth behind closed lips. For a moment, his dad sat staring at him without saying a word.

"What the fuck are you wasting your time talking to that senile old bastard for? Is listening to him more important than listening to your old man?" he asked, then grabbed his old soda bottle from his cupholder and spit tobacco juice in, the brown saliva sinking to the bottom of the bottle.

Howie shook his head, afraid that if he spoke, he would say the wrong thing and trigger his dad. He looked around for his mom. It wouldn't do any good, in truth, but in a moment of fear he did what all kids do: looked to his mom for protection. She must have been in their bedroom watching Wheel of Fortune or Jeopardy, whichever was on this time of night—Howie didn't recall. It was only the two of them in the living room, which usually led to the beatings being worse.

"So... what should we do here then? You know the rules, boy. I don't even want you hanging around those losers anyway. How many times do I need to tell you to play sports like a real man, and stop playing make believe like some queers?"

That made Howie flinch—he hated it when his dad talked that way. If someone wasn't a white male, his dad would typically throw some derogatory word in, making those around him cringe. Being hateful toward anyone different was something he made an art form. It was partly why Howie was attracted to the opposite way of life. His friends were far from normal, which is what he loved about them. He played sports like his dad always wanted him to, and even enjoyed it for the most part. But anytime he tried hanging out with that crowd it only made him realize what he *didn't* want to be like. And besides, he was not even the best athlete in his own small town, what were the odds he would make it someday as a professional? He would rather chase his dreams of making movies or writing horror novels, something that seemed far more reasonable to reach.

"Are you deaf? I asked what should we do here? One minute or one hour, it doesn't make a difference, Howie. Late is late. You think your boss will care what excuses you make some day when you show up late to your job?"

"No, Dad. It won't happen again," Howie said. He wanted to say a lot more, but he knew now was not the time for that.

"Okay then. I feel like being nice this time, so I'm going to give you an option," his dad said.

Howie sighed, knowing neither option would end well for him, and that there was a good chance his dad would end up giving both punishments anyway. But he bit nonetheless, playing his dad's game.

"What are my choices?"

"Well, you either get grounded for a week and lose your stupid little Halloween party next weekend, or you get the belt. You're lucky you even have the option, you little shit. When I was your age, my dad took the belt to me no matter what I did. So, what's it gonna be?"

The Halloween homecoming party at the school was something they had been looking forward to for weeks, there was no way he could lose that. He tried to hold back tears, aware of what he was about to be put through.

"Belt," Howie said quietly.

"Speak up boy, what'd you say? Is your mouth full of shit?"

"I said belt!"

"Oh, now you want to raise your voice? That's an extra lashing right there. Get your ass over here."

Howie couldn't hold the tears in anymore and started crying as he walked toward his dad. Why did he have to be such a mean prick? All Howie wanted was to have a relationship with his dad like a normal kid.

His dad grabbed the belt sitting next to his chair, a belt he didn't even wear but kept in its designated spot for moments like this. He cracked it like a whip with his hands. The sound made Howie jump back, a sound he had heard far too often. The belt was his dad's go to punishment. Something that would inflict enough pain yet remain hidden from the public eye.

"I think I'll throw an extra lashing in for you interrupting one of my favorite movies, how about that?" he asked.

"Dad, *please*. I won't be late again," Howie said, having trouble controlling the crying now.

"Stop your blubbering, you damn baby. You sound like your mom on her period. Toughen up and take it like a man, it's the hard lessons in life that make you stronger, Howie."

As he walked closer to his dad, he vowed to himself that if he ever had kids, he would never treat them this way. If his dad truly loved him, how could he do something like this to his own flesh and blood? Howie closed his eyes and got it over with.

THE CURSED AMONG US

AFTER IT WAS DONE, HOWIE SPENT THE REST OF THE NIGHT IN HIS room. He tried sitting at his desk to draw, but the fresh welts on his backside made it difficult to sit in the pad-less chair. He grabbed his portable CD player and popped in the Godsmack album Cory had let him borrow. Picking up his copy of *IT* by Stephen King, he carefully crawled into bed and hit play on the music, trying to escape reality and read his book. After such an exhausting day, Howie's eyes started to force themselves shut, getting heavier by the second. He had only read three pages before he determined it was going to be an early night and turned the music off. Rolling to his side to avoid the bruises, he closed his eyes and tried to sleep.

The sleep, however, was not uninterrupted. Howie dreamed of running through the woods in the dead of night. Looking back over his shoulder he saw Todd in his killer costume storming after him, machete in hand. He turned back to stare at the woods in front of him and the trees were bending and shifting. Loud cracking sounds escaped the branches as they broke and snapped. Twisted tree limbs reached down, grasping thin air. Howie stopped running, watching the forest changing before his eyes. The woods were a blanket of darkness.

A loud, guttural scream echoed through the forest, bringing Howie to his knees. It was so deafening that he could feel his teeth rattling, tears trickled down his face. He covered his ears to stop the pain. With the distraction of the forest in front of him, he had forgotten about Todd coming up behind him with the machete. Howie turned back and saw that Todd was closing in fast—only he looked different. The white mask was still intact, but the eyes were no longer painted red. In their place were a set of orange eyes, glowing behind the mask like some crazed wildfire. He froze in place, unable to move, when the screaming from the woods ceased. Howie's ears were ringing, and it was unbearable. He squeezed his eyes shut to try to help relieve the pain. The ringing sound stopped, and for a single moment, there was a peaceful silence. The silence was broken up by the voice of a woman.

Come with me.

He opened his eyes, looking around frantically to see where the voice was coming from. Was it in his head? Not only was there no woman around, but Todd was gone as well. Howie looked left to right for any sign of Todd or the source of the voice. The rustling of leaves behind him made him jump. Spinning around, Howie tripped and landed on his backside. He gazed up to see Todd with those orange eyes hidden behind the mask, looking down at him. Behind Todd, the tree branches continued to move and shift. He didn't notice initially, but they were forming a shape behind Todd—whatever this version of Todd was—and that was when Howie realized what he was looking at. The branches were forming hands, and they were reaching out for him, trying to pull him in. He looked back up at the masked face, unable to speak. Todd slowly lifted the machete above his head and swung down violently toward Howie's face.

HOWIE WOKE AT THE SOUND OF HIS OWN SCREAMS. HIS HANDS were up blocking an invisible weapon about to come down upon him when his parents came running into his bedroom. The expressions on their faces were a mixed bag of emotions. His mom looked terrified and sympathetic. Glancing over at his dad, he saw the exact opposite. He looked angry and pissed off.

"What the hell's wrong with you Howie? You better have a good reason for waking me up," his dad said.

His mom looked over at his dad and held up her hands to calm him down. "Bad dream kiddo? You haven't had night terrors since you were like six. What were you dreaming about?"

There was no way he was going to tell them the truth—not after the pact they had all made earlier that night. He had to think of something on the spot.

"Um, I dreamed about a bunch of spiders crawling all over my bed. I know it's stupid, sorry for scaring you guys."

The answer seemed to satisfy his mom, but it appeared to anger his dad even more. His dad looked around the room, taking in all the horror movie posters and Howie's bookshelf which contained numerous Goosebumps and Stephen King books. Howie always thought it was funny where his Goosebumps collection ended and transitioned into Stephen King novels—a sign of when he felt he matured a bit. At this moment, nothing was funny about it though. His dad walked over to his desk and picked up his Michael Myers mask that was placed over a Styrofoam mannequin head. Without taking his eyes off it, he said, "Howie, I think that's enough of this Halloween shit for a bit. You need to stop obsessing over it and focus more on other things—like sports, or getting a job. No wonder you scream like a girl in here at night. Put a poster of Cindy Crawford up on your wall or something. I want these horror movie posters off the wall tomorrow. Got it?"

Howie wanted to plead with his dad, but he knew now was not the time. First, he came home late for his curfew, then he woke his parents up at two in the morning screaming. He would wait until tomorrow and hope that he caught his dad in the right mood.

"Okay, I'm sorry guys. It won't happen again, I promise," he said, knowing full well there was no way to control such things. He could tell his mom felt bad for him, but she also knew whatever his dad said would stand.

"Get some sleep, we've got some chores to do tomorrow. We need to go over to your grandparents' to help put new shingles on the garage roof. I need you at full strength, it'll be a long day," his dad said. He took the Myers mask with him and walked out of the room.

"Wait, that's tomorrow? I was supposed to finish filming a few things with Cory and the guys in the afternoon!"

"What part of grounded don't you understand? Tell the shits to not keep you out so late next time. We leave at eight in the morning, so get some sleep," his dad said, as he walked down the hallway.

His mom said goodnight and turned out the light. As expected, the fresh welts appeared to be for nothing, his dad acting as if he'd chosen grounding. So much for getting an option. Howie's anger was short-lived once his thoughts went back to the awful dream he'd had just moments before. An uncomfortable feeling came over him, a sense that whatever happened out there today was only the beginning.

CHAPTER FOUR

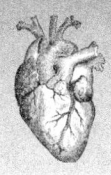

Monday morning in homeroom, Howie searched for his friends to tell them about his dream. Before he could even get a word out, Ryan walked up, his face white as a ghost.

"Dude, something's up. I had the worst dream I think I've ever had last night. It felt so real, Todd was chasing me through the woods—but he was different. Like insane or something man, so weird."

Howie assumed the expression on his face probably gave away his feelings on the topic. He swallowed before saying, "Yeah, I, um... I had the same exact dream. I woke up yelling in my sleep and now my dad wants me to stop with all the horror obsessions. He blames the dream on that stuff—if only he knew."

"We can't say a damn thing, Howie, you know that. Besides, your dad will get over it and forget it was even mentioned. Just give it time," Ryan replied.

"This is the worst time of year to be 'grounded' from horror stuff!" Howie used mock quotations with his hands. "I don't know, man, we have less than a week until Halloween, he better forget quick. That is the least of our worries though. How's it possible we had the exact same dream?"

Ryan was still disturbed by what he saw in his sleep. Howie got the feeling he was not saying something about his version of the dream. Before he could dig deeper, Cory walked up with his bag around his shoulder. He also had a disheveled look on his face. He set his bag on the desk and took a deep breath.

"Guys, I have to show you something. Now's not the time—but let's bounce from lunch early and head up by the ski jump. Remember when I filmed that symbol before shit hit the fan?"

Both Ryan and Howie nodded in agreement, waiting for Cory to continue.

Cory paused a minute before talking, thinking of how to word the information he was about to drop on them. "Well, in all the craziness, I forgot to hit stop, and everything was recorded—I mean *everything*," he emphasized. "It's not all visible, and when the camera hits the ground, the video gets harder to see, but we really have to look at this."

The bell rang, and they all went to their seats as Mrs. Fisher shut the door to the classroom and walked to the front to start the school-day. Howie looked over at Todd's desk and realized it was empty. He felt a gut punch. He shot a look over at the others to try to catch their attention, but their seats were not very close to one another, and he did not want to start his day off by getting in trouble. His ass was sore enough sitting in the school chair, even without the bruises. All he could do was hope that Todd was ok—maybe running late to school. It happened all the time with him.

If Mrs. Fisher noticed Howie staring off into space all morning, she showed no indication. Lunch could not come quick enough.

THE CURSED AMONG US

As they sat at the lunch table, the buzz of all the kids chatting was amplified by the crowded cafeteria. Everyone was excited to talk about their weekends, upcoming Halloween festivities, and anything else enjoyable in their life. That was not the case for Howie and his friends. Cory set his lunch tray down in front of him while Howie and Ryan were already eating their lunches.

"Ugh, how do you eat this crap every day? My dog's vomit looks more appetizing than this stuff," Cory said in disgust. He picked up his chicken patty off the bun; it was a perfect rectangle-shaped piece of meat. "Seriously, look at this! Real meat isn't shaped like this!"

Howie and Ryan forced out a laugh, but they were still bothered by the weekend's events. Cory realized that they were waiting on him to say something about the tape. He also noticed that Todd was still missing. None of them had come out and said it, but they shared the same concerns about him. Todd was the one who touched the grave before the screams came, before they saw something lurking in the distance. Todd was the one chasing them in their dreams with glowing orange eyes behind the mask. Cory had not told them about his version of the dream, but everything they'd explained matched what he had experienced as well. *What does it all mean?*

Ryan cleared his throat to grab their attention. "Probably not the best time to ask, but my mom said I could have a few friends stay over Thursday night to celebrate my birthday. Figured we could play some *GoldenEye* and get some pizzas. You guys down?"

Howie always dreaded hanging out with Ryan. They lived close to each other, so Ryan's mom would often take him for a ride and drop him off to chill without making sure it was okay with Howie's parents first. All Ryan ever wanted to do was watch the same movies and play the same games over and over. To make matters worse, Ryan's house was really small, so they always felt cramped in his room. Unfortunately, they had no choice but to go since it was for his birthday weekend.

"Sure man. Sounds like a good time, I'll ask my parents," Howie said shrugging his shoulders.

"Don't see why not. I picked up *Lake Placid* on video, that could be fun to watch," Cory said.

Ryan could not help but smile, excited at the thought of having his friends over. He shoved the last bit of lunch into his mouth and started talking before he swallowed, "Awesome! I'll let my mom know so she can make sure to order enough pizza. Can't wait."

Cory looked to his bag sitting next to him and his expression went cold. "Okay guys, let's sneak out of here, I need to show you this video and get your thoughts. Maybe I'm losing my mind, but with Todd not here today, I don't think my eyes were just fucking with me."

They got up from the table and set their trays on the counter, then walked out of the cafeteria. Howie's mom always said he looked like the guiltiest kid in the world when he planned on doing something wrong. All they were doing was leaving lunch early, but one would have thought they were planning a bank robbery. He peered around nervously, making sure nobody monitored them leaving. Once they got to the hallway, they made a quick dash for the side exit, entering the parking lot. Some kids wandered around outside, mostly seniors, as they could get in their car to go grab lunch somewhere. Behind the school parking lot sat the basketball courts, football field, and up on the hill next to the school, the ski jump. They headed toward the jump and started climbing the steep incline, heading up toward the woods. The jump was massive, standing at a hundred feet tall. In past years, it hosted ski events and got a lot of media attention. The structure had been brought in from Lake Placid in the late 1970s to a huge spectacle. Over the years it became more of a background display for the school after starting to show signs of rot. The town did not have enough in their budget to spend money on repairs, so it sat towering over the treetops behind the school. It did not take long for students to realize the spot also made a great area to sneak off to for their afternoon cigarette or joint. The guys were relieved to see the slope unoccupied and walked underneath the structure out of sight from of the school grounds below. Cory pulled the camera out of his bag and turned it on. Howie felt another spike of guilt when he saw the cracked screen again.

"Okay, check this out. I know we all saw something in the woods. Part of me hoped it was us using our imagination, but this video proves we're not going crazy," Cory said.

They gathered around and watched the video from beginning to end. Howie couldn't believe what they captured. Everything had happened so fast in the woods that they hadn't been able to take it all in.

In the video, Todd reached down and grabbed a branch from the pile that lay in the tall grass followed by his fake seizure show. What happened next, Howie struggled to make out. Cory had set the camera on the ground, the frame only showing their feet moving around in the tall grass, and frantic voices trying to get Todd back to reality. The argument followed, and then Ryan pushing Todd down into the mound of dirt.

Cory hit pause, and at first Howie didn't know why. Cory pointed to a spot where Todd's hand broke through the soil's surface. What looked like a spark, moving from the ground to Todd's hand, gave off a light red glow. It reminded Howie of how his mom used to turn the lights off and cause a ton of friction on the blankets, creating bright green sparks that popped in his bed. As a little kid, he had always been enamored by it. At the moment however, it was terrifying. How had they not seen that when it happened? And what did it mean?

Howie wanted to say something, but Cory held up his hand to hold him off. "Keep watching..."

The camera faced the woods staring out into the darkness. Once their feet no longer blocked the lens, the wooded landscape became more visible. At first glance, nothing happened. Then the trees started to *move*.

Initially they moved slowly, but quickly picked up speed—more aggressive, like a giant gust of wind was blowing through them, accompanying the screams that came next. Over the next few minutes, they rewatched everything again, from Cory dropping the camera when Howie ran into his back, all the way up to the agonizing screams. What they had missed in the moment was Todd's reaction to those screams. While they all closed their eyes and covered their ears, the camera caught Todd's reaction at a crooked angle. His face did not flinch, showing no emotion. Worst of all, his eyes let off a slight glow, similar to the spark.

"Why the hell didn't you tell us about this earlier this morning, Cory? What the hell man!" Howie snapped.

"I... I don't know. I guess I thought maybe I was seeing things, or thought the camera was busted from the drop. I stopped watching at the part where the figure appeared in the woods, this was the first time I saw the stuff with Todd, I swear..." Cory said.

Ryan stood staring down at the school grounds from the top of the hill. He turned back to them and said jokingly, "Would anyone really miss Todd? He's always a prick."

Howie looked at him disgusted. "What's wrong with you? You think you are any better? The only reason you get picked on so much is because you ask for it. You're like a little chihuahua biting at our ankles all the time, begging us to hang out. And then you spend half the time trying to annoy us!"

Ryan looked away, offended, as though he had no idea how they felt about him. They all stood quiet for a minute. Cory broke the silence as he put the camera back in his backpack.

"Nothing good is going to come out of us arguing right now. Obviously, we're all upset. Let's just chill out."

Ryan had heard enough and started walking back down the hill without them. The bell rang letting them know lunch was over, so Howie and Cory followed. Howie felt bad for what he'd said, but it wasn't exactly false. One trait Howie inherited from his dad happened to be his short temper, and it often led to him saying stuff he would later regret. Sometimes it felt like a competition between Todd and Ryan to see which one could provoke Howie the most.

From this high up, all the students and cars looked minuscule to Howie. The whole town continued going about their business without knowing something awful had been unleashed. Whatever they did in the woods, the feeling had started to sink in that it was more than a scary night in the forest. The sense it would only get worse weighed down on him.

CHAPTER FIVE

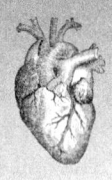

The rest of the day went by in a blur. After seeing the footage, Howie found it hard to focus on actual schoolwork. Luckily, the day ended with film class, which happened to be Howie's favorite. It wasn't just that he got to spend time working on his true passion of making and writing movies. Mr. B, the film teacher, remained very supportive of their dreams. He didn't feel like a teacher to Howie, more like a friend, or a father figure. While his dad would laugh at the idea of Howie wanting to make movies for a living, Mr. B encouraged it. He told them to call him Mr. B because nobody could pronounce his last name. His first name was Paul, so unbeknownst to him, he quickly took on the nickname Peanut Butter. Most considered him a strange man, with quirky mannerisms which often led to students picking on him behind his back, but he saw the true spark Howie and his friends shared in class. For an hour, they could escape the real world, and today of all days, Howie wanted it more than ever.

All things considered, Howie thought Mr. B was alright in his book. Sure, he talked in an energetic voice and his posture gave the look of someone trying to make the back of their shoulders touch, but Howie and the guys learned a ton about filming from him. They would often show him some of the scenes they'd filmed over the weekend, waiting for him to give his thoughts, only to have him give criticism throughout and tell them what needed to be fixed. He got their minds thinking in ways they would not have thought possible on the art of filmmaking. One time he gave them an assignment to make a movie for the semester. The catch —they needed to construct a plot with an object in the room being the center of the story. With only film equipment, their backpacks, and their lunch bags, they found it difficult to get creative. With no idea what to do, Mr. B gave them an example. He took a bag of Chips Ahoy cookies and dropped them on the table in front of Howie and his friends.

"Why are these cookies so important to you?" he asked them.

Ryan said because they tasted delicious. Howie said because his parents did not want him eating a ton of sweets, so when he got his hands on them it felt special. The rest of the class just mumbled among themselves with no real answer. All the students sat there waiting for Mr. B to say something. After a few moments of awkward silence, he pointed at the cookies and then looked at his watch.

"You have until the end of class today to write an outline with those cookies being the focus of your story. Better hurry, only an hour left to come up with something," he said.

They went on to write a ridiculous story about the cookies giving whoever ate them special abilities—with heroes, villains, and everything you would come to expect from a superhero story. The awful movie they made was not the point. The idea to get their creative juices flowing, and structure something around the object alone, gave the exercise its true meaning.

The film room was set up like a college auditorium but on a much smaller scale. The town often held board meetings in the room due to all the filming equipment set up, as well as the television studio, to air the meetings on access television for the town. In the back of the room, a soundproof studio with all the equipment an editor would need to complete a project took up a six- by eight-foot space. In the center of the room, long tables in a U formation faced the front so that all students could be looking at the center where Mr. B often stood as he taught.

He stood, drawing a storyboard up on the whiteboard for the shoot they would be doing on the fall project. As much as Howie wanted to focus on the project, his mind traveled elsewhere. He looked around the class and saw that Cory and Ryan looked just as distracted. Most of the kids didn't take the class seriously, seeing it as a chance to bunk off for an hour every day.

Matt Kelly happened to be one of those kids. Considered the prodigy athlete of Newport, everyone kneeled at his feet when they were around him, including half the teachers in the school. Mr. B was not one of those teachers, often being extra hard on Matt because he rarely participated in class.

Matt sat in the back of the class, up to his usual antics flirting with the one girl, Bethany. This prompted Howie to look over at Cory, who was borderline obsessed with her. Cory's eyes locked on Matt with a look of disgust. Matt oozed confidence anywhere he went, and he acted no different in here. He stood at over six feet tall, worked out religiously, and he always wore the best brands of clothes. Anytime Howie got around him, it made him feel insignificant. While Matt dressed in the newest Starter jacket in middle school, Howie got a knock-off brand that everyone knew was fake. Matt said Howie's parents didn't buy Starter brand for him because he wasn't good enough to be a starter at anything, that he could only wear back-up brands. He gave Howie the nickname 'Backup' during a stretch of fifth grade. Thankfully, the fad wore off with the jackets no longer being the cool thing to wear.

Then there was the time in eighth grade when Matt got a pair of JNCO jeans. It was a strange phenomenon where the cool kids wanted them, as well as the punk rock crowd that decided wearing chains on their pants was as essential as wearing shoes. Howie begged his parents to get a pair of the pants. His dad told him if he could earn the money himself working a job, he would be able to buy them with his own money. The fact that his dad agreed to the idea blindsided Howie. He'd assumed his dad would shoot it down and punish Howie for even asking. That summer, Howie worked at the campground across the street from his house. While his friends enjoyed their weekends, he found himself busy mowing lawns, cleaning out fire pits, and stacking firewood. The owner of the campground, an old man named George, was so impressed with his work ethic that he gave him a bonus. Howie was thrilled, the bonus gave him enough money to buy the pants and finally fit in at school. His mom took him to the store to buy them, and he held them in his possession once and for all.

The thing about his dad was he didn't care what he said before. If he changed his mind, he changed his mind. The next morning before school, Howie came downstairs into the living room wearing his new JNCO jeans. He intentionally did not get the baggiest version of the pants, knowing his dad would flip. The smile on his face went from ear to ear as he packed his lunch and prepared to walk down to the school bus. When his dad saw him in the pants, things went south in a hurry.

"What the hell do you think you're doing wearing those things?" he asked.

Confused, Howie said, "You told me if I worked for them, I could buy them myself, remember?"

His dad looked like the sight of the pants made him want to vomit. He shook his head and stood up from his recliner. "I don't give a shit what I said, I had no idea you wanted to wear something so stupid looking. I should've known better. Take them off, no son of mine is going to be seen dead in those walking trash bags."

Howie argued with his dad to no avail. In the end, his dad made him return the jeans, which was bad enough. What made matters worse, the pants his dad made him wear that day instead. He found an old pair of pants that no longer fit Howie—it was a struggle to even pull them all the way up they were so tight. In one of the most embarrassing moments of his life, his dad forced him to wear the tight jeans to school. He recalled walking down the hall, hearing the laughter from everyone at their lockers as he sped by trying to get to his next destination without being seen. Matt was one of the first to notice him in the uncomfortable outfit, and instead of feeling sorry for Howie, he decided to point it out to everyone in the hallway. Laughter exploded from one end of the hall to the other.

That was one of the memories Howie recalled every time he looked at Matt. It was also one of the many reasons he resented his dad. What kind of parent does that to their kid? The physical abuse hurt, but the mental abuse was soul crushing.

"Howie, I asked you a question," Mr. B said sharply.

Snapping out of his daze, Howie looked up at the whiteboard.

"I'm sorry Mr. B, I had a rough weekend, I'm out of it today. What'd you ask?"

"I'm sorry Mr. B, boo hoo, feel sorry for me, I love you..." Matt mocked from the back.

"Enough of that Matt," Mr. B said, before turning his attention back to Howie. "I asked you about the progress of the script you're writing for the class project we are starting next week. We can talk after class though." He was looking at Howie as if he understood there were bigger issues than the script. Even that simple acknowledgement was more sympathy than he ever got at home.

Ryan chuckled after Mr. B snapped at Matt, and Matt gave him a glare letting him know he'd made a mistake. Ryan looked straight ahead, a big gulp escaping his throat, dreading what would happen to him when class ended. For the remainder of class, Howie did everything he could to remain focused, taking notes until the bell rang.

"Okay, class. We'll continue this tomorrow, remember to study your parts tonight so we can practice the lines tomorrow in class, got it?" Mr. B asked.

Everyone mumbled they got it and shuffled out of the classroom. Howie started to follow them, walking with Cory and Ryan, when Mr. B spoke.

"Hang back for a sec, will you Howie?"

Howie nodded to Ryan and Cory, and they left the room with an understanding the conversation might get personal. When the door shut, Howie turned and saw Mr. B leaning on the table with his arms folded, trying to read his student before speaking again.

"So, you wanna tell me what's going on, Howie? It's not like you to lose focus in here, you're one of the top students I've ever taught." Howie felt a proud sense of worth.

"I'd rather not talk about it to be honest. It was just a bad weekend is all."

Mr. B did not look convinced. "Listen, I know you have a rough life at home. I try to stay out of it, I really do. But if you ever want to talk about it, I'm here, okay?"

Instead of relief, Howie felt a sense of anger inside, throwing himself into instant defense mode. "It has nothing to do with my home life, okay? Stop acting like you know what I deal with."

"Hey, like I said, I try to stay out of it. You're one of the good ones though, I just want to make sure it doesn't impact your education is all." He held his hands up in defense.

Howie bit down on the inside of his gum to stop the tears from forcing their way out. Why was he taking it out on one of the only people to have his back? To actually have someone who cared enough to pull him aside and ask what was up meant the world to Howie and he'd showed his appreciation by snapping angrily. Between his dad hurting him and the nightmare last night, it was hard to keep his emotions in check.

"I'm sorry, Mr. B. You're just trying to help, I get that. The guys and I filmed in the woods this weekend and got sidetracked, I ended up getting home after curfew and my dad was pissed. Excuse my language."

Mr. B smiled. "No apologies necessary. I hope you weren't in *those* woods, Howie. No need to go getting in trouble over something so ridiculous. The town is surrounded by a forest and there are plenty of places to shoot."

He didn't want to lie, but now was not the time to open up about what they saw. He shook his head and said, "No, no. We're smarter than that. Besides, if we went out there my dad would kill—my dad would ground me for weeks."

Another concerning look from Mr. B reminded Howie

THE CURSED AMONG US

he'd said too much already. He needed to leave before he caved and spilled the whole story to him.

"Again, I am sorry for dozing off in class, I'll be focused tomorrow. Thanks for not scolding me in front of the everyone."

"I see big things for you in this industry someday, Howie. We all take our bumps. But it's how you get back up and respond to those bumps that defines you as a person. Besides, if I have to let that big oaf Matt get away with half the crap he pulls, who am I to yell at one of my top students?" Mr. B grinned.

Howie smiled, feeling much better after talking, and walked toward the exit.

"Oh, and Howie? Let's keep that comment about Matt between us, okay? Don't need to be losing my job over someone that doesn't even want to be here," he said.

"You got it, Mr. B. See you tomorrow," Howie said, walking out into the deserted hallway. The timing worked out perfectly, as he did not need anyone seeing what he was going to do next.

✠

HOWIE TOLD HIS PARENTS THAT MORNING THAT HE NEEDED TO STAY at school to work on a project for a few hours and asked them to come pick him up late. The project had nothing to do with school, however. He wanted to spend some time in the library going back through old newspaper clippings. The plan was to learn more about the murders all those years ago to see if he could find any connections. Unfortunately, Ryan had decided not to talk to him after the spat at lunch, and Cory needed to take right off after school, so Howie had the honor of researching in the library all by himself. The good news was that this time of day there would hardly be anyone there to disturb him.

He walked in and saw Mrs. Dalton, the librarian, sitting behind the counter. She was a short old lady who always wore sweater vests covered in some type of pet hair. One time she yelled at Howie to be quiet because he was laughing in the back of the library. What she didn't know was that Howie and his friends had just found the National Geographic section and all the free nudity that came with it. What did she expect a bunch of teenagers to do when they saw a pair of boobs at school?

Today she just looked up, only half paying attention, and nodded before looking back down at whatever romance novel she read under her desk. He took advantage of the lack of attention and briskly walked to the back of the library where all the newspapers remained stored. Only one other student sat in the library, but she had her back to Howie and a portable CD player sitting next to her textbook, lost in the music blasting through her headphones.

Howie went to the boxes of papers, all of them organized by year, and searched for the years 1979-1980. The murders had been reported during this stretch of time, and he knew he needed to start at the beginning and work his way forwards. He recalled the first body being discovered sometime around Christmas of 1979. The town had just survived a massive snowstorm that lasted several days. It took longer than usual to clean up the mess because one of the plow trucks had broken down, leaving Newport short-handed for what would be one of the biggest storms that century. Surrounding towns couldn't really offer any help because they had their own storm cleanup to focus on. To make matters worse, power went out for a good portion of the state as the snow continued to fall in thick, dense blankets. The body would have likely gone much longer without being discovered if not for a random hiker who had gone out in the woods with a pair of snowshoes to kill some time during the town-wide power outage. The snowstorm covered all the blood trail, so it was a stroke of luck—or bad luck if you asked the hiker—that the body was discovered.

The newspaper boxes sat covered in dust after years of sitting in place unattended. Howie dusted off the top of the box to make sure he was looking at the correct year, sending himself into a coughing fit. He saw the years he wanted and took off the cover, finding hundreds of newspapers thickly packed. The old, musty smell of the ancient paper hit Howie at once. They had been sitting here so long that they had all faded to a darker, yellowish hue. Scanning the tabs, that organized by month, Howie located December and picked through until he came to a paper with a headline that looked all too familiar.

BODY OF YOUNG GIRL LOCATED IN NEWPORT TOWN FOREST

Local authorities say a body was discovered deep in the forest of Newport on Saturday afternoon. A hiker out snowshoeing in the woods found the body. Judy Lewis of Newport told reporters the following about finding the body buried under a fresh coat of snow.

"I was walking out in the woods when one of my snowshoes caught on something beneath the snow. At first, I thought it was just some raised tree roots. I went to pull my shoe up and that's when I saw the blood. I moved some of the snow out of the way and saw that my shoe had been stuck on the finger of the body."

Ms. Lewis went on to say she stopped right there and hurried back to town to alert authorities, not wanting to alter the crime scene.

Several police cruisers and officers were on the scene

investigating. One national reporter that stuck around as the police uncovered the body decided to share images—most of which are too violent to reveal—with her network. We have obtained some of those photos which you can see below. When asked about the black stones found around the body with designs painted on them, authorities gave no additional comment, stating they had no reason to believe this was anything more than an animal attack. The victim's chest had been torn open and her heart removed. Police believe this to be the result of a bear or rabid coyote attack.

We will bring any updates as they become available, but for now the police said to be careful in the woods and keep an eye out for any unusual animal activity. As of right now, they do not believe this to be a suspicious death.

HOWIE LOOKED AT THE PHOTOS OF THE SYMBOLS FOR ALMOST AN hour. His hopes felt deflated, as the marks were not the same as those they had seen in the woods. All the pieces he had been trying to put together in his head appeared to be for nothing, and now they were back to the drawing board.

But the black stones *could not* be a coincidence. He was about to put the paper back in the box when something in one of the pictures caught his eye. *Someone* caught his eye to be more specific. In the crowd surrounding the crime scene, none of the faces looked like anyone Howie knew. Even the police officers in the photos, outside of Officer Miller, had long since retired or gone to different towns that offered more exciting work than regularly picking up Tommy the town drunk and throwing him into the holding cell overnight.

One face, however, stood out like a sore thumb. It was Mr. B.

Howie would not have noticed him in the picture when he last looked at these because Mr. B arrived in their town last year to take over the film department. He was a very odd guy, one that got people in town talking when he arrived. Newport was a small town in an area where country music and drinking Budweiser was the norm, so anything that deviated slightly from that was a disturbance to the townsfolk. Mr. B was hired as the head of the local television station due to his vast knowledge of the industry. Some of the residents were not happy with the decision to bring him on, saying that he should not be teaching their kids, that he was an outsider. Howie's dad even considered telling Howie to drop out of the film class and do something different.

Howie was thinking this as he snapped back to reality and saw his teacher standing in the nearly twenty-year-old photo. Standing in a photo that was taken years before he supposedly moved to Newport to run the film department. The feeling of defeat Howie felt minutes ago when the symbols didn't match was now a thing of the past. *Why would Mr. B have been at the crime scene of a murder?*

Looking around again to see if anyone was watching him, Howie decided to hold onto the newspaper for now. He planned to confront Mr. B after class tomorrow and wanted the newspaper as proof. With his heart hammering and about to burst out of his chest, Howie put the paper in has bag, zipped it up, and walked out of the library.

CHAPTER SIX

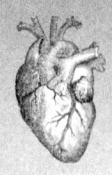

Todd rolled over in his bed and looked at his alarm clock. The light of the clock illuminated his room in the darkness, showing the mess that lay before him. He had to move clutter out of the way on his nightstand—a days' worth of Gatorade bottles, food wrappers, and medicine bottles that his mom forced him to take littered the space. He tried to tell her he didn't think he was coming down with a cold or the flu, but that his head throbbed. It felt like someone had taken a drill and forced it into his temples. At one point, he tried to go downstairs to get out of his room, but he dropped to the floor in pain, unable to see two feet in front of him with any clarity. Things felt much better now, but the threat of the headache still loomed. *How long was I out?*

It felt like days had gone by, let alone hours. The clock said two in the morning. Todd groaned as he sat up in bed and grabbed one of the Gatorade bottles, his throat dry and scratchy. He thought back to all that had taken place over the last few days and shook his head. None of it made any sense. When he'd touched the branches, he'd been joking around and messing with the guys to scare them. He knew that they got annoyed with how often he tried to joke around, but he could not really help it at this point. Anxiety had fueled his daily life for years, and the only thing that helped was when he started making people laugh. Every time he did, the focus no longer remained on his slight stutter and awkwardness. After doing it for so long, it'd became part of his personality, and he could not stop even if he wanted to.

So that's how it started. As a joke. When they got back to their bikes, something felt off. A distant voice spoke within his head. He could not make out what it said, but he sure as hell knew it shouldn't be there. The further away he got from the forest, the quieter the voice became. With the voice diminishing, however, the headache intensified. And then the dreams about killing his friends followed. He chased after them in his killer costume from the movie, only he was not in control of his own body. It was not as simple as being in a dream and having no control, it felt different. Something was forcing him to go after them with the machete in hand.

Todd went to lay back down when the urge to take a piss came over him. He got up and walked down the dark hallway, the cold floorboards creaking under his bare feet as he made his way to the bathroom. With all the liquids his mom had forced down his throat all day, he was lucky he hadn't wet the bed given how long he'd slept. Wetting the bed was something he'd done until a later age than most, and the thought of that happening again brought on a bout of shame. He stood in the dark with his eyes closed, unfocused on where he aimed while he urinated. It was not until he felt a splash on his leg that he realized he'd hit the side of the toilet bowl.

"Shit. Sorry Mom, it's the sickness's fault, I swear," he said to himself, letting out a little chuckle.

He walked up to the sink without flushing. No need to wake his parents and have them come in to check on him again. If he had to answer how he felt one more time, he might actually take a machete to someone, not just dream about it. Looking in the mirror while he washed his hands, he almost jumped back when he saw his reflection. The blue light provided by the moon coming in through the window did not help, but he looked like a ghost. Dark circles under his eyes gave the appearance of someone that had gotten into a fight and had his ass handed to him.

"Woof," he said to his reflection.

Todd walked back to his room and plopped onto his bed. It was surprising how tired he still felt given how much sleep he had gotten today. His dad said maybe he'd finally started growing some hair on his nuts; his mom did not find the joke all that funny.

He started to fall back asleep when he heard a faint sound. A scratching noise coming from the other side of his wall. Todd turned his head to look at the wall that his bed was set against. The noise started at the far side and scraped along, inch by dreadful inch. It moved closer and closer to the middle of the wall, getting louder as it approached. He laid in his bed silent, unable to bring himself to move. The scratching stopped right as it reached his location. He waited for it to start again, only nothing happened. *This is ridiculous, I'm not some little kid afraid of the dark,* he thought.

Leaning closer, Todd put his ear up against the wall and held his breath.

Silence.

The sound that came next was not the scratching sound. It was the voice he had heard out in the woods. The voice telling him to kill his friends.

Join me. Stop resisting. Come...

Todd jumped back, almost falling off his bed. He swallowed the fear down, continuing to stare at the wall and whispered, "Please... leave me alone."

He sat in the same position for a while, afraid to make a sound. She—the voice was definitely a *she*—didn't speak again. The scratching also subsided, leaving his room in the peace and quiet one would expect in the middle of the night. Todd threw off his covers and got out of his bed, tiptoeing over to the window. He wanted to make sure it was locked and close his curtains to keep whatever roamed around out there from seeing in. Inching closer, he took a deep breath and looked out of the window into his yard, half expecting some monster to be standing there. At first, he couldn't make anything out. For a long moment, he stood in place, letting his eyes adjust to the scenery out back. To his surprise, the backyard remained unoccupied. He exhaled and locked the window, turning back toward his bed. His arm bumped into one of his sports trophies, knocking it off his desk. It smashed on the floor, ringing out like a gunshot in the silent house. *Shit, no way that didn't wake my parents up*, he thought as he cringed.

Todd bent over to pick up the trophy—his favorite trophy he received for football last season. It had broken into multiple pieces. After he had gathered all the pieces he stood up, and the headache rushed back. Staring back at him on the other side of the window was the face of a decaying woman, skin covered in mud and blood, her eyes glowing orange. He tried to scream, but nothing came out.

Come with me...

He violently shook his head, sending renewed shots of pain through his temples. He blinked. Nobody stood there looking back at him. Maybe he had a fever, after all, imagining horrible things? Todd hesitantly laid back in his bed, curled up into a ball, and tried to sleep.

CHAPTER SEVEN

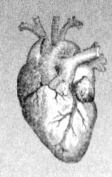

Howie walked into school and dashed towards his locker. He zigzagged through the heavy traffic of kids standing around in the halls blocking the easiest path. Cory and Ryan stood at their lockers chatting about something Howie could not hear over the herds of high schoolers making so much noise.

"Guys, I need to show you something I found last night—"

"Oh, look who it is, did you come back to tell me how you feel about me some more?" Ryan interrupted.

"I... um... no man, I said I was sorry about that. Can we let it go please? We were all stressed out yesterday."

"I'm just busting your balls man, it's all good. You are kind of a prick though," Ryan said.

Howie laughed uncomfortably but was also happy Ryan let it go so easy. His short temper too often had him inserting his foot in his mouth and regretting what he said. With that out of the way, he could focus more on important matters.

"I went to the library yesterday after school to do some

digging on those symbols from the murder scenes years ago. I thought the rocks we saw in the woods looked familiar. Well, there were some similarities, but they didn't match. But it wasn't a complete waste of time going there. I don't know what it means but you need to see what I found in the paper."

He unzipped his backpack and pulled out the newspaper he had taken from the library. Unfolding it carefully to show them the front page and the big picture right in the middle of it. Ryan and Cory came in closer to get a look at the image. It took Ryan a bit longer to make out the faded image, but Cory noticed right away.

"Woah! Why on earth would Mr. B be there?" Cory asked.

In the image, Mr. B stood in the background with a crowd of people looking at the location of the murder. Officers talked in a circle around the spot the body lay covered by a sheet. The picture was old, worn out, and blurry, but his posture alone gave away his identity. He was not doing anything suspicious—but it didn't matter.

"So, what do you think he was doing in Newport twenty years ago? How has nobody else spotted this or mentioned it? You don't think he had something to do with the murders, do you?" Cory asked.

Howie shook his head. "No, they already captured the killer. This is strange for sure, but he didn't kill them. Maybe the reason he teaches here now is because he used to live here and came back?"

"I think if that was the case, we would know. Just look at how people acted when he got the job. They wanted nothing to do with some weirdo who didn't belong in their little bubble to be teaching their kids," Ryan said.

"The guy in the picture is absolutely him. But the only

way for us to find out why he was there is to ask him. What do we have to lose?" Cory asked.

Howie looked uncertain. He had been the instigator, but now he was getting cold feet. He didn't want to alienate the one adult who seemed to stand up for him. "I don't know, do we want to open this can of worms? Like we said, the symbols don't even match, so the shit we dealt with out in the woods likely has nothing to do with these murders."

Ryan looked around and noticed Todd still missing from their group.

"Speaking of, Todd isn't here again today. Now things are getting strange. What sickness goes around in the middle of October?"

Howie shrugged. "I called his house last night to try and talk with him about what we saw on the video yesterday. His mom said he had a bad migraine headache and they run in the family. Said he should be back after a few days."

Howie looked over at Cory for a reaction, but his friend's focus was on something down the hall. Taking a glimpse in the direction Cory stared, he spotted Bethany walking toward them. She was beautiful, with long blonde hair and the cutest dimples that snuck into her cheeks every time she smiled. Had Cory not been basically in love with her, Howie would have drooled over her just as much. It was hard not to stare at her. He turned back toward his locker so he wouldn't get busted by his friends.

"Hey guys! Sorry I couldn't film this past weekend with you, my mom forced me to go to my sister's birthday party," she said and rolled her eyes.

"Oh, it's completely fine, we had plenty of scenes to shoot without you anyway," Cory said.

And it's a good thing you weren't with us out there, Howie thought.

"Well, I look forward to our next shoot! Hey, are you

going to be at the Halloween Homecoming this weekend?" she asked, looking toward Cory.

Cory looked around, assuming she must be talking to someone else. When he realized she was talking to him, he replied, "You know it. Wouldn't miss it for anything. You got a costume picked out?"

"Yes, I'm going as Drew Barrymore's character from *Scream*, my mom even found the same sweater she wore in the movie, and I'll have the portable phone too," she said smiling.

As if Cory could fall in love any more than he already had; his heart was melting now. *Scream* was one of his favorite movies to come out in the past few years.

"That's awesome!" he said.

"Thanks! Well, I better get off to my homeroom, see you guys later," she said and took off.

"I'm so in love..." Cory said to himself as the bell rang and they all filed into the classroom.

THE CLASS SPENT MOST OF THE HOUR EDITING A SHORT FILM THEY had been working on for the upcoming Halloween event at the school this weekend. Howie looked up at the clock and saw the end of class approaching. He was starting to feel anxious at the thought of asking Mr. B about the crime scene photo. While he played out all the scenarios in his head about how the confrontation would go, he felt a pair of hands slam down onto his shoulders and he jumped back to reality.

He turned around to see Matt standing behind him. Matt could have completed his assignments in crayon and half of the teachers would say he picked a wonderful color to write in, so he walked around like he ran the place most of the day.

"Look at the shirt Mr. B's wearing. You think that thing could get any tighter?" He whispered, the smell of old protein shake filling Howie's nostrils.

Howie said nothing when Mr. B responded for him from across the room. How he heard what Matt said, Howie had no idea.

"What's that? You like this shirt? Yeah, they didn't have it in my size, but I just *had* to get it. Maybe I'll give it to you, yeah?"

For the first time Howie could remember, Matt was speechless. He had been embarrassed from this one interaction more than he had the rest of his high school career combined. Howie smiled inside. All the politics in town had no impact on Mr. B or how he handled his class. Matt looked down at Howie and noticed the smile. He had yet to remove his hands from Howie's shoulders and squeezed a bit harder. Howie winced, trying not to show the pain. Matt clenched his jaw and looked in Mr. B's direction like he wanted to knock him out.

"Fucking weirdo," he muttered under his breath.

"I'm sorry, did you say something Matt?" Mr. B asked.

Matt gave a fake smile and nodded toward the clock.

"Said I think it's time to *go*." He walked over to his desk and grabbed his bag, storming out of the classroom.

Everyone had been holding in their breath, afraid to laugh in front of him. That would surely end in a beating outside of school at the end of the day. The majority of kids in the class were considered geeks, losers, and unpopular. When Matt joined, they were all upset. Seeing him put in his place made it all worth it. Students filed out of the classroom as the day came to an end. Howie felt his heart pounding as he thought about the confrontation that

THE CURSED AMONG US

inevitably faced him. Cory and Ryan walked over to Howie's desk, and they all waited together for the room to empty. With everyone gone, Howie pulled out the newspaper and cleared his throat.

"Um, Mr. B? We just... we wanted to chat about something with you we came across. Do you have a minute?"

Mr. B gave them a perplexed look and motioned them over to the larger desk in the center of the room. They all sat in the chairs around the table, all of them except for Mr. B. He climbed up on to the table and sat with his legs crisscrossed.

"What's up, dudes? Is it about what just happened with Matt? Sorry if that upset any of you, I'm sure I'll be hearing from his parents," he said with a smirk.

"No, actually. That was super cool seeing him put in his place for once. We wanted to show you something that is confusing us," Howie said.

"Okay then, how can I help you guys?"

Howie grabbed the newspaper and unfolded it. Mr. B knew what was on the paper as soon as he laid his eyes on it. He hopped off the table and grabbed it from Howie's hand.

"Why do you have this?" he said sounding uneasy.

"We... I went to the library last night to do some digging on the murders from years ago. I wanted to get a look at those symbols they found near the bodies—"

Mr. B cut him off.

"What the hell would you be looking into that for, Howie? That stuff should really be left to rest. The last thing this town needs is that crap being put in their brains again. Just let it be," Mr. B snapped.

Cory did not appreciate the tone their teacher had used and stood up.

"No, we didn't come here to answer your questions, we

came to *ask* them Mr. B. Why were you at the scene of a murder twenty years ago before you even lived in this town?"

Mr. B walked over to the door of the classroom. He looked out through the window into the hallway and pulled down the shade so nobody could see in. It was obvious he was nervous about something, debating what he should say to them. Evidently, people didn't like it when you uncovered an old photo showing them at the scene of a dead body.

"Guys, I'm going to tell you some things that may seem a bit hard to comprehend. But before I do, I need you to promise me this info does not leave this room. I could be fired and sent packing. Agree?" he asked.

They all nodded in agreement. Mr. B continued, taking their word for it.

"Okay. I will start by admitting to you, me coming to this town wasn't an accident. I had a fairly solid resume under my belt in the film industry; coming to some small town and running their local television station wasn't exactly a dream job. I'd been monitoring the town for years, and this opening was what I needed to get closer. You see, back in the late seventies, I was involved in a documentary that focused on black magic, the occult, and those who practiced it all. There had been reports of it in the New Hampshire area, specifically in this region." He was pacing up and down the aisle with his hands in his jean pockets, looking around.

"I hadn't been here long enough to get a cup of coffee let alone talk with anyone before the first murder happened. The snowstorm didn't help the situation either. You better believe they questioned me when that picture was in the paper. I told them I was working on a new documentary, and when they investigated who I was, they believed me. There was nothing pointing to me as a witness. Hell, even the local authority passed on talking to me after the Feds told them I was harmless. I saw the symbols around the victims well before they made the information public later on. I tried to tell them what the symbols referenced. They were sigils, used in witchcraft for protection. Now, who would try to put a protection around a dead body? Over the next few months, I hung around the area trying to track down the source of the magic. I had to be discrete because I didn't want police to get pissed off at me or think I did have something to do with it. The bottom line is this—I started out working on a documentary about the subject and got sucked into a serial killer investigation. At the time, all I could think about was money and how set I'd be if I was the one to uncover the killer. The longer it was drawn out, the more I realized I didn't care about the money. It became an obsession. Fast forward to when Henry Black was arrested, when the police said they had the killer in custody. I—are you guys following me so far? I feel like I'm rambling..." Mr. B looked at each of them.

They all nodded, and he continued his story.

"What police don't want anyone to know is that I went to the agents when they said they had the killer. I *told* them none of it made sense, that Henry showed no signs of being a killer. That he couldn't have done those things and they were missing something. As soon as I brought up black magic, forget about it. They told me to go back to Hollywood and make movies if I wanted to live in a dream world." He shook his head in disgust, and then continued on. "Henry didn't help the situation. They asked where he hid his wife's body, and he wouldn't say a word about the location. All he said was he couldn't tell them because if they found her, there'd be much bigger problems. They chalked it up to a psychopath talking nonsense and gave up searching for her body after a few weeks. I, however, did not give up. I've searched the surrounding woods for years, looking for any sign of a grave. If everything I think is true, I believe he knew of greater dangers than he was letting on. That Jessica was just part of a much bigger problem. He was protecting us from her."

Ryan could not hold in his anxiety anymore and had to speak up.

"Why're you saying, 'protect us from her', Mr. B? The killer was captured and is now dead. He killed his wife after she found out he was the murderer, it was all over the news back then—"

Mr. B held up a hand to stop him.

"Because that's what they *wanted* everyone to believe so the story would die. What they didn't know, or didn't *want* us to know I should say, is that Henry was not the Black Heart Killer—his wife was."

CHAPTER EIGHT

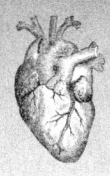

After the nightmare of the previous night, Todd felt surprisingly better when he woke up. Bits and pieces of his dream still roamed around in his head, but they were quickly fading with each waking minute. His mom insisted he stay home one more day to be safe—to make sure the headaches did not reoccur. When his parents went to work the house was his and his alone. He planned out the events of the day in his head while eating breakfast. A day full of PlayStation, junk food, and sneaking into his dad's porn stash was just what the doctor ordered. Everything had been going according to plan until just after lunch time. He made a grilled cheese sandwich with extra cheese and butter, grabbed a soda from the fridge, and sat down to watch some television while he ate. Flipping through the channels, Todd stopped on the Jerry Springer show. This episode titled "A Threesome Gone Wrong" had just started. *Jackpot,* he thought to himself. He grabbed the soda and chugged down half of the can in one gulp. His parents surely would have told him to have better manners, but what they didn't see wouldn't hurt them. A large belch bubbled up in his chest, exploding out of his mouth. Letting out a laugh, he set the can back down on the coffee table in front of him and settled in to listen to what Jim Bob did wrong to get both girls pissed at him in the bedroom.

A fight broke out before poor Jim Bob could explain himself to the audience. Chants of *Jerry, Jerry, Jerry* passed through the studio audience as the two girls ripped at each other's hair and clothes. Todd saw a rip in the shirt of the hotter of the two girls, exposing part of her bra. He sat up and looked closely, trying to get any glimpse that would not get blurred out on cable television. Before he had a chance to get a better look at her, Jerry looked at the camera and said they would be right back. *Oh, come on!*

The excitement of seeing the girls ripping their clothes off triggered another thought in Todd's head. He better hurry if he wanted to check out his dad's private porn stash. His dad hid them in the most obvious spot too. He probably thought he was being sneaky, but Todd had found them in his parent's closet one day while looking for a home video they had filmed a few Christmases' back. The gift Todd found that day was far better than anything he would open on Christmas morning.

He grabbed the remote off the coffee table and turned the television off when something caught his eye. As the screen went blank, Todd could see the reflection of a figure standing behind him at the couch. The features remained indistinguishable, with the room peppered by daylight shining in from the living room window. Fear glued him in place, afraid to make any sudden moves. The thought occurred that his eyes could be playing tricks on him, that he would turn around to see nothing there. That thought, however, proved to be false. Before he could get up, the voice thrust itself back in his head.

You have not done what I have asked of you... You must get back to the woods, remove the remaining sigils and set me free...

"Who are you?" Todd whimpered.

Do as I say boy. Do not worry about who I am. Or what I am. If you want to live... if you want your family to live, do as I say...

Todd cleared his throat and decided to turn around to face this thing head on, but something froze him in place. He briefly felt paralyzed and could feel himself being held with gravity forcing itself down on his shoulders. When he looked back at the television screen, he tried to scream out at the top of his lungs but only a small whimper escaped. This thing now leaned over the couch right above him, her hands holding Todd down on the couch. Tears slowly slid down his cheeks, his body shaking in terror. Glancing at his shoulders, there were no hands touching him. How was she doing this? It was as if she was in some in-between world, able to control him, but only seen in reflections. He knew physically she was still buried out in the woods.

Do you understand what must be done?

"Y-y-y-yes. Go to the woods a-a-and clear off the rest of the grave so you can be free," Todd whispered.

Good boy. You must go before anyone else discovers me. Before they prevent it from happening. Now GO!

Todd lowered his head like an abused dog that knew it was about to get hit. She was so loud in his head; the headache was promptly back. He realized the force no longer pushed down on his shoulders, yet he was still mentally frozen in place, afraid to move. After what felt like minutes passing by, he looked back to the T.V. screen and saw there was nothing behind him. He looked at the clock to gage how much time he had before his parents got home. If he hurried, he could get to the forest area—assuming he could remember exactly where the grave was located—pull off the remaining pieces of the symbol and get home before they were back from work. They both worked late tonight, which gave him a little more time to get the job done. Hopefully after he did this, she would leave him alone for good. It felt like wishful thinking but bringing himself to think about what he could possibly be unleashing onto his town was something he had to bury deep in the back corner of his brain.

CHAPTER NINE

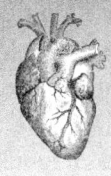

AFTER PAUL DROPPED THE BOMBSHELL ON THE KIDS ABOUT THE Black Heart Killer being the convicted murderer's wife, the room went silent. While Todd rested at home, immersed in Jerry Springer, they were all sitting on a family drama a heck of a lot more serious than an unsuccessful threesome. How could the authorities not have known about this? The truth was the case had been botched in more ways than one back in 1979. But Howie knew with cops it was often black or white, there was no gray area when it came to so-called facts. They could not bring themselves to believe a bloodthirsty witch, who practiced black magic, had savagely killed all the victims—not when they held proof that Henry killed his wife after a thorough search of his house. They found several victims' belongings inside the Black residence. Besides, nobody had ever reported any strange behavior from Mrs. Black in the neighborhood, only from Henry himself. Neighbors said he had been acting strange lately, coming and going at odd hours of the day. Their neighbor across the street, the boy's English teacher Mr. Carl, called the cops because he saw Henry walking into his house with blood on his shirt. He said that Henry looked discombobulated and scared, like he did not want to get caught. When the police arrived, they blocked off the surrounding streets with New Hampshire state troopers, and a S.W.A.T. team was called to take Henry into custody. The former chief of police said in an interview with the local paper that it had been a risky situation to go in with all that firepower without firm evidence, outside the testimony of the neighbor across the street. Granted, Mr. Carl also coached the high school football team and had a lot of pull in the town after back-to-back state championships. If it had been anyone else calling it in, it likely would not have been taken as seriously.

The police found numerous objects hidden throughout the house that supported the theory of Henry as the killer. An ancient dagger with dried blood on it, a map to the forest where the bodies had been found, and of course the bloody clothes Henry wore earlier that morning when Mr. Carl called the police. It was as iron clad a case as you could get. Then, when Henry would not tell them where he put his wife's body, it sealed the deal. The evening news ran a breaking story that night about the killer being captured, and once his name was revealed, they coined him the Black Heart Killer. Newport could breathe again, knowing their small town was now safe.

Something Henry said to the police stuck with Paul though. Not everything was black and white to him like with them. When the authorities asked Henry why he killed his wife, he answered, "I didn't kill her, she was already dead. She was not my lovely Jessica anymore, she turned into... *something else.*"

An alarm went off in Paul's head when he read that. Knowing they found all the evidence, that exposed a household that had delved into the occult, he pieced it together and felt almost certain Jessica Black was the true killer. Paul spent years looking for the burial site, determined to prove his case.

Now, this group of kids stumbled upon her grave by *accident*. If not for the seriousness of the situation, he would have laughed at the irony of it all.

Before the kids left the classroom, Paul filled them in as much as possible about how dangerous this situation was. How to protect themselves if what he thought was about to happen unfolded in their little no-nothing town. Of course, he would not say anything to the police, at least until he obtained proof of the situation. Otherwise, they would lock him up in the same high security nut house that Henry Black had been locked up in. They said he suffered nightmares about his wife, and raved incessantly about her.

The students couldn't stay long, afraid they would arrive home late and get in trouble. But before they left, Paul was lucky enough to get the location where they found the grave site. Part of him felt a little resentment towards them for finding the location he had been searching for so long by accident, but he needed to put that behind him. He had searched that area of the woods many times and come up empty handed, so that was on him.

Later that evening, Paul locked up the front door to his house, double checking his bag to make sure he'd packed everything he needed in the woods, including some protein bars and water in case he got lost. He made a point to record his thoughts on his Dictaphone before he left, just to be safe. The last thing he wanted would be no record of his investigation before he went out there. If something happened to him, he wanted to be sure a backup existed. Paul walked over and hopped on his bike. Next, he put his backpack on, followed by his helmet, and strode off down the road, crunching fallen leaves under his tires as he sped off.

It was a nice autumn afternoon, the sun still beaming down strong, making the day unseasonably warm for late October. Getting to the site and back out of the woods before dusk would be of utmost importance. He needed to be quick, the last thing he wanted was to be deep in the woods with the possibility of being stuck out there with a monster.

He still did not quite know what he was dealing with. Paul researched a broad swathe of the occult for years. But this situation felt so different from anything else he had ever seen or read about. He knew Jessica Black was involved in witchcraft, but that did not fully explain the murders. Of all the witches Paul had met over the years while filming his documentary, there were only a few instances where a bad seed tried to stray from their usual craft. Most of them wanted to be left alone to study their practices and go on living their lives the way they wanted. No, it was not as simple as a rogue witch going on a killing spree, it had to be much deeper than that. If his theory proved correct, Jessica Black not only studied witchcraft, diving deeper and deeper into that world, but had become bored with her studies and like an addict needing a stronger drug, had searched out *more*. Witchcraft led to black magic and satanic rituals. Somewhere along the line, he believed that she had become possessed by a demon and created some horrifying hybrid. That was just his theory, but the pieces added up.

Just after 5:00 P.M., he approached the entrance of the cemetery. From what Howie had told him, it took them almost an hour to get to the gravesite. It was partially a guess, considering they had stopped to shoot multiple scenes along the way.

Despite his fear and excitement, it was hard not to be

concerned about Howie's situation at home. Paul had intentionally taken him under his wing, hoping to help guide the kid to a better future, one he knew Howie would excel in. The poor kid's dad sounded like a real peach, at least from what he was able to pry from Howie about his homelife. When this was all over with, he planned to look into the situation some more, discreetly, so that he wouldn't lose the trust he'd built up with Howie. But it was very evident that things were physical in the Burke household.

Paul coasted up to the mouth of the graveyard and came to a stop. The scenery really was a sight to behold. The tar walkway into the main entrance of the cemetery led to a massive field of gravestones, the grass around them covered in orange and red leaves as autumn was hitting its peak. Had it been any other day, Paul would have taken out the camera to snap a few shots. It presented the perfect image for a homemade calendar. But he did not have time to revel in the beauty. He parked his bike at the edge of the forest and began a brisk walk into the woods, praying that he was not too late. Paul got so caught up in his destination, he missed one key thing that would have likely saved his life. Over in the deep grass, behind the cemetery shed, lay a kid's bike hidden in the brush.

☨

Todd had no trouble finding which direction to head when he got in the woods. The closer he got to the cemetery, the louder her voice got in his head. And the voice would not let him get lost. It was like having a demonic GPS telling him each and every turn. The pain was unbearable, forcing him to stop multiple times on his way. Every time he stopped, she reminded him stopping wasn't an option.

Thinking ahead, he had grabbed his backpack on his way out the door, knowing he still had some snacks in there from the movie shoot over the weekend. The weight of the bag surprised him as he got deeper into the woods.

Knowing that stopping generated a one-way ticket to a migraine from hell, he unzipped the bag while walking, feeling around for a bottle of water. Instead, he felt the hard plastic outline of the mask, followed by the sharp blade of the machete. *No wonder the bag weighs so much,* he realized. Cory was supposed to take the props home with him but must have forgotten with all the commotion going on while they escaped the woods. The backpack had gone untouched since then. Careful not to get cut by the blade, he found a bottle of water and pulled it out, taking a big gulp to quench his dry throat. The deeper he got into the woods, the more shocked he was that they had ever found their way out of here in their panicked state of mind. It felt as if he was being swallowed by the forest. The only sounds he could hear were the cracking and snapping of dead leaves and branches under his feet. He had to be close, he had been walking over an hour and nightfall approached.

Put the mask on...

"Huh? Why the hell would I do that?" he asked confused.

Someone else is out here with us... You may need to handle it boy...

"Can't you just scare them away? You had no problem doing that to us when we were out here."

I said do not question me, did I not? Put the mask on and do as I say...

He wanted to ask why again, but he didn't want her to put a vice-like grip on his brain once more. Hesitantly, he pulled the mask out and gave it a look. It felt ridiculous to go along with, but he also did not want to be seen by anyone out here, so he pulled it over his head and continued. The site was just ahead; she made sure he was aware of it.

PAUL WAS THINKING THROUGH THE SITUATION THE BOYS RAN INTO while he hiked deeper into the woods. They told him everything that happened. The shrieking they heard, the figure off in the distance of the woods—all of it. She did not attack them or come close. They had also avoided digging up the grave, and as Howie mentioned, they left the stones in place. So, how had they seen her? Was she somehow manipulating their minds? The thought of that possibility made his stomach churn. As far as he knew, she still lay buried in her grave, still guarded by the obsidian stones. He clung to this information as a trivial hope that he still had time to prevent this situation from getting out of hand. Had she been at full strength, she would have surely attacked them, even being far outnumbered. At full power, she could kill the whole town, one by one—and she likely would do just that if given the chance. While he did not know everything about what type of powers she possessed, the fact that she could rip a chest open with her bare hands said enough. He also knew that you could not truly kill her—*her* being whatever demon had taken over Jessica's body all those years ago. Whatever Henry did to get her out in the woods this far, and then bury her under what sounded like a protection sigil from the kid's description, was a miracle. It also explained why Henry refused to tell the police where he'd buried the body. Henry had known all he did was protect them from her temporarily, but he hadn't eliminated the threat. That was why it was so important to get out here and make sure the gravesite never got discovered by anyone else.

The sunlight was starting to creep down behind the trees, earlier than he hoped. There was no way he would be getting out of here before nightfall at this point. Paul considered himself an outdoorsman, often going on hiking trips and camping off the grid. He had not come unprepared for that possibility. Everything he needed—besides a tent—was packed in his bag, including a flashlight. Normally he would have been marking the trees as he went, limiting the chance of him getting lost, but he could not take the risk, as it would lead anyone who'd decided to come out here right to the very gravesite he wanted to hide. The clearing they'd told him about was just up ahead. As he understood it, from here he needed to go toward the next set of pines; the grave would be in the tall grass to the left. Adrenaline had the blood pounding in his ears as he approached the wooded area. Before going in, he stopped to make sure he'd packed the black obsidian stones. If she was stuck in some in-between phase right now, the sigil would protect him if she tried to get close enough to possess him.

With his heart thundering against the inside of his chest, he walked into the opening and approached the grave. Right away, he could see the area the boys were talking about. Tall grass intertwining with bushes hid the conspicuous mound of dirt, which had largely been covered by growing weeds over the past twenty years. The protection symbols were still there, but a few had fallen off to the side and cracked from the weight of someone stepping or falling on the area. Crouching down, Paul carefully moved aside some of the undergrowth to get a closer look. Henry really did a good job of secluding this out here—nobody in their right mind would come this far into the woods.

He set his bag down by his side and was about to look through it when he heard a commotion behind him. Already on edge, he whipped his head around. There was nothing there. Odds were it was a squirrel or chipmunk running from one tree to the next, trying to find an acorn to bring home to their stash before winter arrived. He stared a minute longer, making sure nothing was going to jump out and attack him. An overwhelming sense of dread overcame him—he felt like he was being watched. The silence out here could be so peaceful in the right situation, but right now all it did was amplify the unsettling feeling.

Paul turned back to the grave and prepared to lay down the new obsidian stones he'd brought with him, planning to place them around the mound of dirt in a circle. Another snap of a tree branch—this time off to his right, stopped him in his tracks.

"Hey! Whoever's out there, the joke's over. Time to come out and show your face," he said in an unconvincing tough guy voice.

He stood and slowly walked toward the area the sound came from, quietly reaching down to grab ahold of a thick branch that'd broken off a nearby tree. The branch would be useless as a weapon, he could feel the rotted hollowness of it in his hands. It should have weighed a lot more in his grip based on its size. He knew one swing would break it to pieces, but he hoped it could at least scare off anyone out here trying to spook him.

Up ahead, leaning against a tree, he saw another backpack. He looked around again, checking once more for any sign of life out here. Nothing. *What the hell?* he thought. The backpack was open on the ground. Paul kneeled and started looking through the contents. All the bag contained were a few drinks and snacks, nothing more. He flipped the bag around and saw the name of its owner. It said TODD SEYMOUR, grade 9 on the name tag. A puzzled look crossed Paul's face. Todd had been missing from school the last few days, his friends said he had been acting funny after they left the woods. What was his bag doing out here still? He must have left it in a moment of panic when they ran out of the forest.

Paul started digging through the bag some more, looking for any sign of recent activity. Nothing stood out to him, so he closed the bag. As he went to get up, he heard heavy breathing over his shoulder. A shadow soon followed, blocking out the remaining sunlight that had been poking through the canopy. He jumped up and turned around—and came face to face with a masked man holding a machete. No, not a man, a *kid* he thought. The mask was white and expressionless—the only spot of color was blood red dripping down from the eyes.

"What the hell—" His question was cut short as the machete came swinging in at him. He stuck up his arm and the blade sliced through his forearm with ease, sending his left-hand thudding to the ground. Paul screamed, clutching the stump, dropping his mock weapon. Blood squirted out where his hand used to sit, spraying all over the forest floor in front of him, plastering the maniac's shoes. He could feel himself getting groggy. The kid charged at him again, lifting the blade up. Paul picked the branch back up in his other hand and swung it blindly, striking the arm holding the machete. The branch fell to pieces on the ground, leaving him defenseless. The one thing it had done in his favor was buy him some time. The machete fell to the ground and the killer bent over to pick it up. Paul kicked him square in the chest, sending the kid stumbling down into a cluster of bushes.

With every ounce of energy left in his body, Paul forced himself to run deeper into the woods, clutching his severed arm to his chest. Against the hazy, darkening sky, black branches writhed like the tendrils of a monster, scratching Paul's skin as he blasted through them. He needed to get to safety, get medical attention, or he was going to die. It was now approaching full dusk, and this far out the sun struggled to remain relevant. For a man in his mid-fifties, he was in great shape. Every weekend he would run half marathons, and once even completed the Boston Marathon after months of rigorous training. The difference is he did all of that with both hands attached to his body—without pints of blood squirting out all over the ground, ruining the perfect display of fall colors. He could not run much longer. Sprinting got his heart pumping full throttle, which was expediting the rate of blood loss. Unsure if the killer remained hot on his trail, he stopped for a minute. *So lightheaded,* he thought as he leaned against a tree to hold himself up.

He pulled off his belt and attempted to tie it around his arm in a makeshift tourniquet. Continuing on felt impossible. There had to be a spot where he could try to hide, get out of sight until this nutjob left the woods. He pressed his face against the bark, trying to become one with the tree, the rough surface scratching the side of his face. His mouth was so dry; all he wanted in that moment was a tall glass of water to help him keep moving. He peered around the side of the tree, looking for any sign of the lunatic following him. Instead, he saw a trail of blood leading right to the tree he hid behind. This spot would not work, he needed to find darkness where the blood couldn't be seen. Pushing himself off the tree, he took off at a jog, oblivious to the branches scraping along the side of his face and body. Up ahead, he could make out what looked like a steep decline, and headed in its direction. He arrived at the edge and again looked back over his shoulder to see how close the killer was.

He saw the outline of the figure approaching.

Hopefully the kid couldn't see any more than he could.

The edge of the hill looked to be much further down than he was hoping for. The slope dropped close to ninety degrees, making this more of a cliff than an actual hillside. There was absolutely no way he would be able to climb down with one hand. He looked side to side for any other options, but it was either try to get down this slope, or head back in the direction he had come. He felt himself beginning to hyperventilate and took deep breaths to try and calm himself.

Tree roots poked out of the side of the hill most of the way down. He needed to treat it like one of the rock-climbing trips he had done many times throughout his life. Granted, he didn't have a harness or rope—or a left hand for that matter. Paul sat down on the ground, rolled over onto his stomach and slid his feet down over the side. His wound slid across the ground when he pushed himself back, and a rush of pain shot through his entire body. Tears escaped the corners of his eyes, rolling down his cheeks. He clenched his teeth together trying not to cry out.

Feeling around blindly with his foot, he found the first tree root and planted his foot on it. With his right hand, he felt around for something to grab hold of. At first there was nothing, filling his stomach with dread. He made it all this way only to get stuck on the side of a hill and bleed to death. Reaching down a little further—as far as his right arm could extend—he felt the tip of another root and dug his fingers into the dirt around the gnarled wood to get a better grip. With darkness swallowing the forest, Paul began his descent down.

Todd continued looking for Mr. B in the dark. His parents were certainly going to beat him home now, and he was never going to hear the end of it. But he had bigger problems than getting grounded. After Mr. B had kicked him down, he'd thrown up inside his mask, unable to get the image of the machete cleaving off his film teacher's hand out of his head. He hadn't wanted to swing the machete, but her voice had boomed so loud in his head, forcing him to do it.

He slowed as the edge of a cliff appeared up ahead. Todd had lost sight of Mr. B awhile back and hoped that he went in this direction. At first, he followed the blood trail like he had done when he was younger, hunting with his dad and uncle. They shot a deer and forced Todd to follow the trail looking for the poor animal. He felt awful. They told him to stop being such a pussy and go find it. He located the deer further in the woods, limping along, trying to survive. The animal had turned its head and he felt its black eyes staring right at him. Todd felt so bad for the thing. At that moment he decided to run a different direction and get his dad and uncle off the trail. They were pissed at him later that night for not finding it, but he liked to think that he'd helped the animal survive. That was exactly what he wanted to do for Mr. B, but unlike his dad and uncle, she was not going to let that happen. Her voice buzzed like a static being cranked to full blast in his head. He winced, shaking his head from side to side in an attempt to rid his mind of her. But she would have none of it, she continued chipping away at his will to live. It was as if he was a passenger in his own body, fully under her control anytime she decided.

Find him... Kill him...

Climbing down the side of the cliff was becoming increasingly difficult. Paul glanced down into the darkness. At this height, he likely would not die if he slipped and fell, but he sure as hell would break some bones. His fingertips were losing grip the further down he went. He searched for anything that could help him survive. As if on cue, he spotted a hole in the side of the hill. It looked as if a washout during a bad rainstorm formed this indent underneath some exposed tree roots. The biggest issue would be getting to it. The area was on his left side—the side he had no hand to grab with—so moving in that direction seemed borderline impossible. Still, he had no choice if he wanted to stay alive. If he died out here, nobody would be able to tell the town how to defeat the evil force that stalked them. He spent years of his life studying the practices of witchcraft and black magic. Nobody else in this shithole would have the slightest clue on what to do in a situation like this.

Paul reached to the left with his damaged arm, feeling around for a place to hold on. Everything they said about losing a limb and having the sensation of it still being attached was true. His brain wanted him to grab on with a hand that wasn't there. The wounded end of his arm grazed against a protruding root, sending a shot of pain down his entire arm. A scream forced its way out before he could tell himself to hold it in, and he hated himself for it. He froze in place, hoping the arrival of nightfall still hid him from the monster above. Paul could not hear any sounds coming from the killer's direction.

He waited.

When he felt safe enough to continue, he bit down on his shirt preparing for the pain he was about to endure and shoved his damaged arm through the tree root to latch on, hooking his elbow around it. As he bit down on his shirt with all the force he had, he reached over with his foot and found a spot to plant. After a few more unbearable steps, he reached the opening and dropped himself down into the hole. He took deep breaths, trying to calm himself. The air inside the makeshift cave had an old earthy smell to it, reminding him of the damp crawlspace in his basement growing up. As a child, he would pretend to crawl in and hide from evil monsters that lurked in the dark of the unfinished storage room. He wished he was playing make believe now, but instead of pretend monsters looking for him in the dark, a real psychopath was on the loose.

In the moment of stillness, the pain really set in. The adrenaline he had pumping through him from the run in the woods temporarily relieved some of the suffering, but now it was here to remind him that he had, in fact, just had his fucking hand cut off. He felt around in the darkness, finding piles of damp autumn leaves everywhere. A thought came to him, one that could save his life. He couldn't see anything outside of his hiding spot, but he had no idea if the kid would be able to see him in here when he descended the side of the hill.

Paul pulled as many of the leaves as he could close to his body, covering himself the best he could. If he could hide himself long enough to catch the killer off guard, maybe, just maybe he could make it out of here to warn the town.

The crunching sound of approaching steps alerted him. He listened closely to see how far away the noise was coming from. The movements were much closer than he was hoping; it sounded like the masked kid was right on top of him. He held his breath, his entire body tense. Paul focused on the opening, waiting for his chance to pounce.

A few leaves dropped from above the cavemouth, followed by some small rocks and dirt. Paul could now see the outline of feet coming down from above. The killer dropped to the edge of the opening, standing only a few feet in front of Paul. Heavy breathing came from behind the mask; the killer was clearly out of breath from the strenuous climb down the side of the hill. He stood there, frozen in place.

He can't see me, I need to stay still and wait for my shot, Paul thought.

The kid finally moved, turning to look outside of the hole. He stared down the cliff-side, looking for his future victim. It was now or never. Paul lunged out from the leaves, colliding into the unsuspecting boy. The kid let out a startled cry as they both flew out of the hole, airborne for a brief second before slamming down onto the hillside. Paul's busted hand banged into a rock when they landed, and for the third time in less than an hour, he felt the worst pain he had ever felt in his entire life. They tangled with each other as they rolled down the side of the hill before going airborne again, this time much longer. Paul landed first, his back crashing down onto the ground below, knocking the wind right out of him. His head smacked off the ground with a sickening crack, leaving him dazed. Most of the killer's weight landed on top of his body, adding to the impact. He looked up and saw the attacker also hurt by the collision. Through blurred vision he could make out the kid's arm bent at an unnatural angle; a blade of broken bone pierced through the forearm, and he could hear the kid's screams as he rolled off, clutching his arm. Paul had a brief feeling of satisfaction—it seemed fitting this little bastard broke his own arm after cutting off his hand. The satisfaction was short-lived, as he lifted his head and looked down to see the machete sticking out of his stomach. Blood was soaking his shirt, spreading at an alarming rate.

Rolling to his side, he grabbed the handle of the machete, preparing himself to pull it out. Before he summoned the courage to do it, the killer crawled over to him, crying out in pain. That voice behind the mask—it sounded familiar. The kid grabbed ahold of the machete handle and yanked it out. Paul's eyes rolled in the back of his head; the pain was unbearable. The killer stood over him, machete in hand. His broken arm hung limp at his side. Crazed eyes stared down from behind the mask.

"No, I can't do it, please don't make me," the kid said, talking to himself.

He placed the machete under his arm and lifted the mask off his head. The face on the other side of the mask was Todd's, and he looked heartbroken. Staring down at Paul, he grabbed the machete and shook his head.

"I... I'm so sorry Mr. B. She's in my head. I can't make it stop... I'm sorry."

Before Paul could respond, Todd swung the machete down, right into his throat. Paul spit out blood, his head hanging on by a few remaining threads. With everything turning to darkness, his last thought faded with it. *I was too late.*

CHAPTER TEN

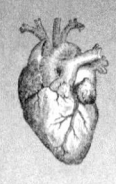

Ryan sat at the dinner table shoveling down the food that sat in front of him. He was in an extra chirpy mood tonight. His mom had picked him up from school and they had gone shopping at Wal-Mart to pick out all the snacks and party favors for his sleepover. On the menu tonight was one of his mom's go-to meals when they were running short on time. A plate full of Spam and mashed potatoes covered in butter and gravy. Ryan sat, daydreaming about the party and having the guys over, when his dad spoke from his love seat in the living room. His dad was pushing four hundred pounds and had trouble sitting at the kitchen table on the small wooden chairs, so he usually ate his dinner in the living room over a food tray.

"What's this about you guys out in the woods where we told you not to go, kid?"

Ryan looked over at his mom confused—he'd told her in confidence about being spooked out there. She peered away, knowing it would hurt Ryan that she had said something. He had made a deal with his friends to keep his mouth shut, but he always told his mom everything. As close as he wanted to be with the guys, he knew deep down how much he annoyed them. All he wanted was to be accepted, to enjoy his childhood like he saw all the other kids doing at school. He had not been blessed with the best genes growing up—he was overweight, wore thick glasses, and to top it off, he lived in a small mobile home out in the woods. While the gang did not treat him the way he thought friends should treat one another, they at least put up with him. His mom, however, she was his best friend, and his dad was a close second. Being an only child made things lonely around the house, but it also allowed them to spoil him—spoil him the best they could on their income, that was. Every video game system a kid could ask for sat in his room on his cluttered dresser. He had a desktop computer, something most kids his age could only dream of having. All of that could only be an escape for so long though. Ryan felt if he was the one who had been absent from school and acting strange, nobody would notice. He felt himself trapped in this cycle every day of his life—get picked on, make jokes about it to try and show it didn't bother him, get everyone to laugh. Rinse and repeat. But what they didn't know was how he felt every night when he came home, often crying in his bed, ashamed of who he was. Why did anyone care that he was overweight? Did it truly make them feel that much better about themselves to pick on him any chance they got?

He looked at his dad, ashamed he'd hid the story from him. But more than anything, he was angry with his mom for breaking the trust between them. He would have told his dad when he was ready. His parents did not lay many rules on him. There was no curfew. No bed time. He could eat whatever snacks he wanted, all while playing and watching the most violent videogames and movies he wanted. One of the very few rules they had given him—stay out of those woods.

"Sorry I didn't tell you Dad. I... I was going to, but I didn't want you to get mad at me before my party this weekend and ground me. I swear we didn't plan on going out that far, we just lost track of how long we were walking."

"Ryan, I'm not mad. I'm disappointed more than anything. We intentionally try to be loose with you so you can enjoy being a kid. But those woods... they're not a place kids your age should be playing. Who knows what might be out there? Did you know there were missing persons reports that never got solved after the Black Heart Killer was captured?"

Ryan shook his head, and his dad continued.

"I know you play all those violent games shooting and shit, but this is real life. The stuff you could find out there could scar you for good. The police say they searched all through the woods and that any bodies the killer buried out there were all discovered, but you weren't around back then. There's more to the story than you could grasp at this age. Someday I'll talk to you about it."

"Dad, since we're talking about this now, I want to ask you about the killer. I know you guys don't like to talk about it much, but... were there any people back then that thought maybe that guy Henry didn't do it?" Ryan asked.

"Huh? No Ryan. Why would they think that? The guy was caught with evidence in basically every damn room of his house. We just felt the police seemed to close the case awful quick."

"It's just—" Ryan started before his dad cut him off.

"That's enough of it. We all want it behind us and staying out of those woods is part of it. We live in New Hampshire for Christ's sake—it's filled with forests. If you guys really need to film in the woods, you can use this area. The worst thing you'll run into out here is a couple of rabbits fucking," his dad said with a smirk.

Ryan laughed. His dad always knew how to turn his mood around and make light of everything. He wanted to talk more about what they saw out there, what they heard. In time, he would bring it back up. The thought of using the woods around his house for the movie got him excited. If his mom and dad talked with the other parents about what he had told them though, he wasn't so sure they would want him involved anymore.

"Guys, I'm sorry I went out there. It won't happen again, I swear. Can we please not tell the other parents about this though? The guys would hate me if they knew I told you."

Ryan's dad grunted. "I suppose there's no harm in keeping it between us. But you do it again, and how your friends treat you will be the least of your worries, got it?"

"Yeah, Dad, I got it."

"Okay then, let's drop it. You wanna go watch *The Thing*? That's next up on the list for our horror movie marathon. Not much time left before Halloween's in the rearview and we're looking on to Christmas."

"You know it! Best movie of all time in my eyes."

"Easy does it, kid, nothing tops *Evil Dead*. *The Thing* is close, but Bruce rules them all," his dad said. He got up from his loveseat and rubbed Ryan's head.

"Let's go, dude. I'll get the popcorn ready. Time to see you piss your pants in fear."

CHAPTER ELEVEN

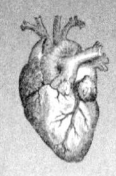

Howie sat on the couch with his PlayStation controller in his hands. He was playing a game of *Madden* against his dad. His attention could not stay on the game, however. All Howie could think about was the conversation he'd had with Mr. B after school. It was hard to believe his story, about what he thought happened in those woods, about the possibility that Jessica Black could be the true serial killer that haunted Newport.

Mr. B told them he planned to check out the grave site after school, and that he would report back to them tomorrow with what he found. It felt good to have someone to turn to who believed their story. Even if they caved and told their parents, they would more than likely tell the kids to stop watching horror movies and grow up. As much fun as Howie had playing video games with his dad—really the only thing he enjoyed doing with him—they did not have the type of relationship where he felt he could talk to him about anything personal. Howie kept it all bottled inside, leading to minor panic attacks any time something stressful in his life came up. His instinct reverted to try and forget about anything that became an inconvenience in life, bury it in the back of his mind and try to pretend it never happened. He couldn't help but feel the only time his dad could stand him happened to be when they played video games together.

His mom stood in the kitchen, washing dishes at the sink. The clang of a pan snapped Howie back to the television. He hit a button on the controller, passing the ball down the field, the player on the screen caught a deep touchdown pass and Howie fist pumped in the air.

"Jesus Christ, can you keep it down out there?" his dad snapped toward the kitchen.

Howie's dad had the tendency to be a poor sport when he got beat, often blaming anything else besides his lack of skills for causing him to lose. It was kind of funny until he stopped and realized that his dad often took it out on his mom. She typically sat minding her own business, cleaning all the dishes the entire family just spent time eating off. Eating a dinner that she also cooked for them while they sat there playing more games. Howie looked up and saw the game not even to half time yet. Normally he loved sitting here playing, but tonight he only wanted to go to his room and study the old paper he picked up from the library some more.

The house phone rang, and they all looked over at it. Howie's dad paused the game shaking his head.

"Who do you think would be calling this time of night?" his mom asked.

"It's not going to answer itself, pick the thing up and find out!" his dad snapped.

She walked over and picked the phone up off the charger and answered. Howie watched her face, curious if it related to their trip in the woods. He would not put it past Ryan to tell his mom and dad, which would in turn lead to a call to the rest of the parents. His mom started to say hello, but someone cut her short.

"Oh, my goodness, Jody!" she said covering her mouth. The expression on her face showed one of shock.

"Okay... Yes, we'll be right over. I'll tell them now... okay. Jody, I'm so sorry," she said.

Howie had no idea what she could possibly be talking about, but Jody was Todd's mom. Did Todd finally tell her what they found? Had his headaches gotten worse? It killed Howie to know what was being said on the other end of the phone. His mom set the phone down and cleared her throat.

"That was Todd's mom. Howie, have you talked with him at all today?"

"No, he wasn't at school the last two days. His mom said he had a bad headache. Why, what happened?" His windpipe felt like it was closing, the anxiety hard to control.

"They um... they got home from work and Todd was missing. His bike and backpack are gone, so they think he went somewhere while they were at work. But he still isn't home. I told her we'd be right over to help look for him," she said.

Howie's dad sighed and set the controller down on his coffee table.

"The little shit probably went out to get himself into trouble and didn't see what time it was. I never trusted that kid," he said shaking his head.

"Well, we have to go look for him. How would you feel if your son was out there missing?" his mom asked.

"I'm not fucking going anywhere but bed, he'll turn up. These kids never faced a curfew so they think they can come and go as they please. You see why we make you come home by a certain time Howie?"

Howie looked down, avoiding confrontation. Every

ounce of him wanted to argue with his dad but he knew better. He would never listen to what Howie had to say. It was his way or punishment, and it was as simple as that. Before he could respond, his mom saved him.

"Howie let's go. We'll go help the Seymour's look for your friend," she said while giving her husband a nasty glare.

Howie got up and walked outside without another word.

What could Todd be doing? Howie thought to himself. It was now becoming impossible to ignore what they saw in the video. The light shooting from the ground up through Todd's hand only lasted a brief second in time, it didn't feel like something that carried any relevance... Until now. He could hear his parents arguing inside as he opened the car door and got in. A sense of dread filled his lungs like a cloud of dense fog. Something was wrong, and he knew it. He closed his eyes and took deep breaths, telling himself to stay calm. *Easier said than done,* he thought as his mom came storming out of the house.

CHAPTER TWELVE

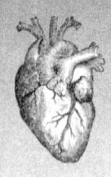

Todd finally made it back to the top of the hill after struggling through the climb with a broken arm. His body collapsed to the ground, forcing him to lay there for a moment and think about what he'd done. He looked down over the side, getting one last glimpse of Mr. B lying on the ground below. He felt grateful it was too dark to see the blank stare of his teacher numbly looking back at him. All he wanted was for this voice to get out of his head—to leave him alone and let his life get back to normal. It wouldn't be easy to forget the things he'd done tonight, but he hoped eventually he could get to the point where he could avoid being haunted every waking minute. Coming up with a story to explain his broken arm would be easy enough. He would just tell his parents he tried to go out, thinking he felt better, and fell off his bike.

The thought of his arm brought the sense of pain back to reality. He had broken bones before playing sports, but nothing to this extent. As bad as the arm hurt, the headache drilling into his brain took the attention off the broken bone. No normal person could have climbed that hill with a bone sticking out of their forearm. Todd knew how bad it must be and avoided looking down at all costs.

Now, free me...

His head was on the verge of exploding like a baked potato in a microwave. It was as if the more impatient she got, the more pressure she cranked into his head. Todd leaned over and vomited on the ground. Everything hit him all at once. He'd just *killed* someone. Not just anyone, but his teacher, who he respected and enjoyed talking to. His entire body was shaking. He had a severely broken arm, and it felt like someone was using the sides of his head as a drum set. *Thump, Thump, Thump*. Over and over. Todd sat up and started crying uncontrollably.

"Why? Why are you doing this to me? I just want my life back... please!"

If you want your life back, release me NOW!

Todd grabbed the sides of his head, forgetting all about the broken arm as he did. He jumped up and walked over to the grave site. It was now pitch dark, and he could not see more than a few feet in front of him. He came to the bag Mr. B had left behind and searched through its contents. It was going to be important that nobody found the belongings. In the bag's contents, he found a flashlight—which he took out to provide some light on the way home, and some black stones. They were like the stones that circled the top of the grave when he and his friends discovered it. He was not sure why, but he felt they must be important and put them in his pocket. The bag would have to wait—there was no more holding off what he felt forced to do. Not if he wanted his brain intact rather than scrambled like the commercial from health class about the brain on drugs.

He stood over the grave, heart pounding in his chest. *What am I about to set free?* The thought of what she could do once she got out terrified him. Todd realized he hadn't brought anything to dig the grave with and sighed. He reached down and pulled off the black stones that remained, followed by the branches that had been crafted into a makeshift cover to hide the location. With his functioning hand, Todd began to dig through the mound of dirt and weeds. *This is going to take forever,* he thought. After a few more moments of rigorous digging, he got up to see if anything in Mr. B's bag would help move things along faster. Before he could get to the bag, a mind-bending scream came from the direction of the grave. Todd shot back around to get a glimpse, and what he saw shook him to his core.

A monstrous hand with long, jagged fingernails forced its way up through the dirt, clawing at the pile. He let out a scream and backed up, afraid to get any closer. The hand was covered in soot, the skin a decaying, gray color. Next, a second hand shot up from the hole. Both hands sat in place for what felt like an eternity. The moon shone through a lattice of leaves to give the ground an ominous glow. Todd did not advance, too frightened to make any sudden moves. He gulped at the air, trying to slow his breathing enough to listen for any more sounds. A low, visceral growl escaped from the hole, making his stomach churn. *What the fuck is this thing?*

The growling stopped, leaving the forest in complete silence. Todd took a hesitant step toward the grave. Before he could even take a second step closer, she shot out of the hole at a speed unlike any he had ever seen. The figure flew by him, knocking him to the ground on the way. Todd tucked his broken arm to his chest as he fell, landing flat on his back. It knocked the wind right out of him, sending him into a coughing fit. He did not get a good look at her before she made it out of sight. Not that he wanted to see—the hands had been terrifying enough. He took more deep breaths, trying to dim the pain and catch his breath. Todd got up, listening for any sign of where she went. He walked back through the woods in the direction he'd chased Mr. B, the static sound in his head driving him forward. A soft slurping sound off in the distance caught his attention. It made sense that after years of being buried in the ground she would need some water. Every morning when he woke up, the first thing Todd went for was the glass of water by his bed to wet his parched throat.

Looking around, he did not see her anywhere. The sound reminded him of his dog lying on the floor, licking between its paws to clean the day's grime away. It sounded like the slurping was coming from over the hillside.

As he approached, Todd grabbed the flashlight at his side. He neared the hillside, waiting to turn on the light. The slurping sound got louder as he drew near. He turned on the flashlight, aiming it down over the side of the cliff. All the horror movies in the world could not prepare him for the scene below. She crouched over the limp body of Mr. B, his dead eyes staring straight up into the sky. His chest was torn open, blood splashed across the ground. *No. No. Please no.* The monster held the heart of his former film teacher, her claws digging firmly into the organ. Todd screamed at the top of his lungs and fell back, the flashlight flying out of his hand, smacking off the ground. He only saw the back of her head, but that was enough to know what she was doing. She was *eating* the heart. Todd grabbed the flashlight off the ground and ran toward home, never looking back.

CHAPTER THIRTEEN

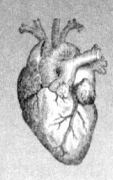

Howie sat on the couch in Todd's living room, listening to his mom frantically talk with Jody in the kitchen. They were trying to come up with the best plan to go looking for him. Todd's mom was a mess, crying, struggling to finish a sentence. The police had left the house moments before, and they would be out making rounds in town to look for Todd. They saw that his bike was missing, as well as his backpack. When one of the police officers asked if Todd could have run away, his mom lost all control she held onto. None of it made any sense to her. She told them when she left for work that morning, Todd said he felt better and would go back to school. He had been in a great spirits and could not wait to see his friends again. The officers assumed it must be a case of cabin fever after being stuck home for a few days, that he likely went out to get some fresh air or maybe see a friend. That prompted Jody to call all the parents and see if he'd stopped by, clinging to any shred of hope.

Howie was scared. He debated breaking the promise he'd made with his friends and telling the parents about their trip to the woods. It was becoming increasingly harder to keep that secret with everything going on. Not that either set of parents would have listened or believed him anyway. He didn't know why his mom even brought him; she told him to wait in the living room while they talked. She more than likely wanted to protect him from hearing anything a fifteen-year-old should not be involved in, but with how loud Jody talked, the conversation could be heard at the opposite end of town.

They'd checked all his friend's houses, the library, even the park. Everything came up empty-handed. Howie wished Cory and Ryan were with him so they could talk about where Todd might have gone. It had only been a few days since they last saw Todd, but it felt like weeks.

The conversation in the kitchen had gone silent outside of sporadic sobbing. Howie picked up the remote to the television and turned it on, hoping to drown out the crying. As much as he wanted to hear what they were saying, the guilt felt like a pair of cinderblocks placed on his shoulders. There remained a very high likelihood that Todd's disappearance had something to do with the strange altercation at the grave site, and no matter how hard Howie tried to force that thought from his head, it continued to dance around in his brain.

He numbly flipped through the channels, trying to find anything that would take his mind off the nightmare. With Halloween less than a week away, there were ample amounts of scary movies on to choose from. He settled on the *Poltergeist*, watching as the Freeling family yelled at their daughter to run towards the light. Howie had watched the bloodiest, gorefest movies growing up, yet the *Poltergeist* was one of the only movies that scared the hell out of him. For the moment, he focused his attention on the scene in front of him. That was until Jody screamed from the kitchen, yelling Todd's name. Howie jumped off the couch and ran out to see what'd caused the commotion.

Standing at the entrance of the kitchen door was Todd. He remained there a few seconds before collapsing to the floor, clutching his arm to his chest. He appeared to be in some kind of trance, insensitive to the uproar going on around him. He looked straight down at the floor; his body shaking. Howie noticed blood all over his clothes, triggering another bout of panic. *What did he do?* Todd lifted his head and looked at Howie before he turned his attention to his mom, who had run over to him. Those few seconds of eye contact burned a hole into Howie. A blend of guilt, pain, and fear had shone on Todd's face.

"Oh, my dear lord, what happened to you, Todd?" Jody cried as she put her hand on his shoulder to comfort him.

Todd did not answer, he just leaned his head on her and closed his eyes, tears pouring down his face. Howie stood frozen in place, staring at his friend. Reality hit him—their lives would never be the same. Todd's bone poked through the skin of his forearm, dried blood ran down his arm, stopping at his elbow. His pants and shoes were covered in blood as well. Everyone stopped talking for a moment, an uncomfortable silence filling the room, giving Todd time to get his emotions intact. He was a mess, undoubtedly in shock. So was Jody. Howie's mom walked over to the house phone.

"We need to let the police know we found him Jody. I can call them so you can be with your boy. And then we need to find a way to let Donnie know, since he's out there looking still. Todd needs to get to the hospital as soon as possible. Get him there while I call for you, okay?"

Before Jody could respond, Todd looked over at Howie's mom.

"No. Please, don't call the cops. I... I really don't feel like being questioned by them right now. I just need to get my arm taken care of and rest. Please. I'll talk to them another time."

"Todd, hun. She has to call to and let them know we found you. We don't need to have them talk to you right now. If we don't tell them, they will be out looking for you still," Jody said.

Todd hesitantly nodded, climbing to his feet. The pain in his expression was clear as he moved his broken arm. Howie's mom talked with the police station as he walked out the door behind Todd and Jody. The chill of the evening air hit him as soon as he got into the driveway. He felt fortunate they didn't have to be out in the woods searching for Todd in this weather. Jody looked back at her son; Howie could only imagine what was going through her head right now.

"Are you ready to tell me what happened today?" she asked.

"I... I went out for a ride and fell off my bike going down Fellow's Hill. I tried to catch myself on the way down and my arm landed first," he said.

"Oh god, you're lucky you aren't dead Todd! That explains all the blood on you, and what took so long to get home. You poor thing," his mom said.

Howie saw right through Todd's story. He needed to get Todd away from his mom so they could talk about what *actually* happened. Whatever story he told his parents and the cops, Howie knew there was a very good chance the version he got would be much different. He needed to think of something to get her away.

"Jody, it sounded like they might want you to come on the phone for a sec to let them know Todd's condition," Howie said.

"Okay, you keep this kiddo company. I'll be right back,

Todd," she said rubbing his cheek with the back of her hand on her way by.

As soon as she went back to the house, Todd knew what was coming. Howie wasted no time getting right into it.

"Man, what the hell happened to you? Please tell me it had nothing to do with that shit in the woods?"

Todd let out a nervous laugh, hesitant to respond. *What is he not telling me?* Howie thought.

"I'm so sorry... she left me no choice Howie."

"No choice for what? What'd you do?"

It was hard deciding what he should tell Howie—what to tell the truth about, what to lie about. So, he decided to tell him everything. He had to get it off his chest. He took a deep breath and got started.

"When we were out in the woods, and saw what we saw, something happened to me dude. At first, I was just messing with you guys when I played around with the grave site, pretending to get electrocuted or something. Just being stupid you know? When we heard the screams, and saw the figure in the woods, I heard something in my head. Something...*awful*." Todd looked over Howie's shoulder toward the house to make sure his mom was not coming back yet before continuing.

"I heard a voice in my head. She was telling me to do some bad things to you guys. I was so scared from it all that I ignored her at first. I thought we all could hear her talking until I realized you guys weren't reacting to what she was saying."

"What did she want you to do to us?" Howie asked.

"I'm pretty sure you can guess without me needing to spell it out. Anyways, after we left the woods, it got worse. She was in my head—it was driving me crazy. All I told my parents was that I had a terrible headache, which was true. But I didn't mention her voice. The more she talked to me, the worse my head felt. It was like a drill spinning into my temples. Whatever we saw out there in the woods, it wasn't her. It was like a ghost of her or something, I don't know..." he said.

Howie was getting confused; he knew they did not have much time before their moms came out to get them.

"What do you mean it wasn't her? I'm pretty sure we all saw someone in the woods looking back at us."

"I know because I freed her from the grave tonight. She forced me to—"

Todd didn't get to finish his sentence as his mom came rushing out of the house, heading right to her son.

"Okay, let's get you taken care of, Todd. Oh, my goodness, I can't believe we made you wait this long. That must be so painful," she said with concern.

When his mom got in the car, Todd looked back to Howie. "All I know, is that she's getting closer to town, Howie. And she is getting stronger—I can sense her more every day. We need to stop her *now!*" Todd whispered.

He gave Howie a look as if to say "we will finish this conversation later". As Todd got into the car, Howie started toward his mom's vehicle, ready to follow his friend to the hospital. He noticed Todd's bike and backpack were sitting at the side of the house.

"How the heck did you get that bike back here with one arm?" Howie asked.

"You would be surprised what you can do when a monster's controlling your head," Todd said quietly. He shut the door and looked blankly out the window.

CHAPTER FOURTEEN

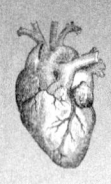

Tommy stumbled along the train tracks, taking in the brisk night air. He was starting to really feel the buzz of alcohol. He knew the town labeled him as the drunk, but he had no control over the situation. All anyone saw when they looked at him was a sloppy, dirty bum. But they had not seen the man he was before he came to this town. He spent the last fifteen years wandering the streets, paper bag in hand. It was very cliché—he knew the paper bag coupled with his dirty clothes looked like the exact definition of town drunk.

Years ago, he had a wife and family to go along with a successful career running a local gas station in his hometown. He loved the banter with his regulars when they came in every morning for their coffee. Just thinking of those moments brought a smile to his face—at least until the smile caused pain in his decaying mouth. As good as the cheap bottle of whiskey made him feel, his teeth rotting out of his skull over the last few years had started taking its toll on him. All the alcohol, drugs, and bad diet had finally caught up. Dental care was the least of his worries when he lived off welfare and struggled just to avoid becoming homeless.

Everything had been going so well for his family until a day that started out like any other. He went into the store early to open and get the cash register ready for the day. The sound of the car doors shutting outside still haunted him every time he thought of that dreadful morning. He assumed a few of the regulars were coming in early for their coffee, but he would not be opening the store for another hour. Two masked men walked into the store; the bell rang to let him know someone had entered. He looked up from the register to see both pointing guns at him. They asked him for the money in the register. Tommy considered himself a proud man, and he would do whatever it took to prevent them from taking the money. He just happened to be sitting on a larger than normal pile of cash from the weekend rush in town and hadn't had the chance to bring it to the bank yet. So, he resisted. Under his register, a gun sat in a holster. Tommy never actually thought he would need it in such a quiet neighborhood, but it provided a security blanket. When he attempted to grab the gun, one of the thugs saw what he was doing and shot him in the shoulder. Tommy flew back into the cigarette rack behind the counter and fell to the ground, cartons of cigars and cigarettes piled on top of his unsuspecting body. The man who shot him came over to see if he'd killed the clerk, looking over the counter to find Tommy grabbing his gun and pulling the trigger, shooting the masked man right in the head, dropping him dead on the store floor.

Tommy hunched over, holding his wound to stop the bleeding when the other assailant yelled out in a desperate panic and fled the store without taking the money. In that moment, Tommy thought he had saved the day and taken a gunshot for it as a lifelong reminder. Not until the police arrived and pulled the mask off the victim did he see he'd shot and killed a kid. A kid that happened to be friends with his own son. This realization sent Tommy into a downward spiral. An addiction to painkillers after years of dealing with shoulder pains from the gun shot only multiplied the freefall. Sprinkle in a bit of his family hating him for killing his son's close friend, and it made a toxic cocktail indeed. It did not take long before he got kicked out on his own. The family of the dead kid had taken him to court and Tommy spent all the money he had invested into the store on legal fees. This led to losing the store to the banks—which also happened to be where Tommy had been sleeping after his wife kicked him out, leaving him on the streets with nowhere to go. So, he moved to Newport following the events, in hopes of starting over and finding a more affordable living situation in a small town where the cost of living would be a fraction of what he had been used to.

It became a nightly ritual to think through all the events that led to this moment. Just like it was a nightly ritual to down an entire bottle of cheap liquor—the brand or type didn't matter—whatever he could get his hands on would do. Tommy walked along the track, using it as a makeshift balance beam. He blew his breath out, watching it create a cloud in the frigid air. As he struggled to maintain his balance, he held his arms out to the side, thinking it would help him stay up right. On each side of the train track, miles of forest stretched in both directions. The solitude of being out here where nobody else could bother him really had a calming effect. He stepped off the track and stared up at the stars. *What did I do to deserve this life?*

Looking straight up threw off his balance, causing Tommy to stumble back and land ass first on the metal track.

"Son of a bitch!"

Pain shot up Tommy's tailbone and he rolled over to grab his precious bottle, which had dropped to the ground, dumping most of its remaining contents.

"Son of a *bitch*," he said again, almost laughing at himself.

He sat up and took one last swig of the bottle, making sure every last drop was accounted for. When nothing remained, Tommy looked at the woods in front of him and yelled "Fuck you!" throwing the bottle as hard as he could. The glass smashed off a tree and shattered to pieces. The throw sent a shot of pain up his shoulder—another reminder of the shot that'd got him in this situation to begin with. He gently massaged the front of his shoulder, trying to calm the burning sensation pulsing in his deltoid. A rustling sound in the woods up ahead caught his attention.

"Hello? Who's there?" he said in a slurred voice.

It was hard to see at nightfall, but he thought for sure he saw movement sprinting through the woods. He squinted, trying to get a better look. Maybe it was the booze messing with him, possibly a deer had spotted him and run for safety. Tommy stood up and walked toward the treeline to get a closer look.

Snap.

There it was again, movement off to the right. He knew his vision was no longer top notch, but with his blood alcohol content pushing maximum capacity, it was a struggle to see more than a few feet in front of him. An eerie feeling of being watched struck him at once, sending goosebumps into a frenzy on the back of his neck. *Screw this,* he thought. If he could take down a pair of thugs with guns, why the hell would he fear some rabid fox out in the woods?

"Hey...you fucking rodent, come here and say that to my

face!" he shouted. "Yeah, that's what I thought, now leave me the hell alone. These are *my* tracks at night."

Tommy shook his head and continued walking down the path, only the stars giving off a faint glow to the darkened landscape. Up in the distance he could hear a train heading in his direction. The sound was barely audible outside of the sporadic bellowing of the whistle, indicating it must be a good distance away still. In his younger days he would have considered trying to hop the train and having it take him to whatever final destination was in store—get out of this hell hole of a town. At this stage of his life, however, it hurt to walk, let alone try pretending to be some stunt double.

A thought occurred to him just then. Maybe he should just lie on the track and end it all—the misery, the depression. But he knew deep in his unrelenting misery, he could never do that. He was a fighter. A fighter that'd lost everything, but he was determined to get his life back on track. As soon as this bottle wore off, he was going to start over tomorrow. Clean himself up, get his act together, and go look for a job. Maybe he could even get a job down at the gas station in the center of town and work his way back up to the top. Yeah, that sounded like a nice plan. That was just what he would do.

A loud shriek came from the woods. The sound startled Tommy and he tripped over the train track. He tried to catch his balance, but gravity got the better of him. His head smacked off the metal, sending a cracking sound into the night. The pain that followed was excruciating. Tommy tried to sit up, but his vision went blurry, causing a bout of nausea to kick in. The sound of the train was getting closer. It wasn't just the train that he heard though. At the edge of the tree line, footsteps approached. He was having trouble seeing even a few feet in front of him. The train advanced, getting louder and louder. Whoever stood in front of him, maybe they could help pull him off the track before it was too late. He squinted, trying to clear his eyes enough to make out the approaching figure.

"Please, help me! I hit my head... I need help getting off the track!"

Something was wrong. The silhouette of the figure approaching him was *off*. This was not someone coming to help him, that now seemed obvious. Tommy closed his eyes and said a prayer. He had faced so many obstacles in his life. Dying on a train track was not something he would have expected to mark down on the wasted life bingo card. He owed it to himself to put every last ounce of life he had left into rolling off the middle of the track.

When he finished his prayer, he opened his eyes. What he saw sent shivers down his spine. An abomination towered over him. A human-like figure with orange glowing eyes gazed down at him. She was hunched over, her arms dangling down low to the ground. The train was not too far off now; he was running out of time to escape before he was crushed under five tons of metal. But at that moment, the train was the least of his worries. He would almost welcome it compared to the alternative in front of him.

She inched closer, leaning over his body. Her matted down hair smelled of the rot of years of neglect. He could sense the predatorial rage she carried inside. *What the fuck are you?* he thought.

The front-lights of the train came into view as it rounded a corner two hundred yards to his left. The loud whistle of the train blasted out into the night as it chugged along. Tommy gave one last effort to sit up and escape. Before he'd made it more than a foot, the creature swiped her jagged nails across his face, slicing through the skin like a sharp knife cutting into a medium rare steak. Tommy let out a scream, falling back again. Blood gushed out of the wound that started at his cheekbone and advanced down to his neck.

"Please let me go, I'll give you anything you want! *Anything*!"

A force unlike any he had ever felt went off like an explosion inside his brain, and then he heard what had to be the Devil inside his head.

What I want, is your HEART!

Tommy tried to struggle free—she did not feel overpowering in any way—but in his drunken condition, a toddler could hold him down. The thing started clawing at his chest as the train now approached within a hundred yards of them. She dug and clawed with a ferocious tenacity, trying to tear her way into his soul. Tommy screamed at the top of his lungs for her to stop, but she was only going to stop once she got what she wanted. She let out a blood-curdling shriek of frustration. Claw marks raked his chest and blood poured out through his ripped shirt. The creature reminded him of a dog trying to dig a hole, dead set on getting a bone buried deep underground. The light of the train threw illumination over the figure hunched over him, clawing at his upper body. Her facial features remained hidden by her knotted hair, but he could see razor sharp teeth as they snarled at him. They were covered in a mix of dirt and blood; the stench coming from her mouth was revolting.

Chug. Chug. Chug.

Tommy realized he was about to either get ripped apart by this monster or crushed by a speeding train. He opted neither was how he wanted to go out. Forcing his arm free, he grabbed ahold of her wrist and tried to pull it away from his chest. Her skin felt clammy and damp. She ripped her arm free from his grasp and swung down with full force across his throat. Blood sprayed onto her face. Tommy's eyes bugged out as he tried to take deep breaths while also choking on his own blood.

Chug. Chug. Chug

Tommy jerked his head to the side, looking at the oncoming train. It was very close now, but she did not seem to notice. If he was going out this way, so was she. He latched on to her arms with a tight grip. She screamed in his face, blood and spit dripping down onto his forehead.

"You stu... stupid bitch," he coughed out.

She looked over at the train, which now closed less than twenty feet away, its whistle blasting out. Tommy held on with all his strength as she fought to get free. His strength was dwindling, he felt his grip loosening. She tore one of her arms away, slamming her fingers down into his eyes, grabbing his skull like a bowling ball. She snapped his head to the side, breaking his neck instantly. As the train smashed through his limp body, she leapt off him at the last second, screeching in rage, in unison with the train whistle, as she ran back into the woods. She would have to wait to feed.

CHAPTER FIFTEEN

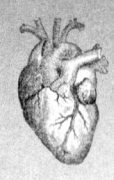

THE WARM WEATHER THAT HAD BEEN HANGING AROUND LATER than normal this fall had finally decided to take off for the winter. Howie walked to school on the chilly fall morning, his breath painting the air with each exhale. He walked like a zombie, overtired from the night before. They had spent a good portion of the night at the hospital, comforting Todd's mom while he remained in surgery. Todd's arm had been shattered in multiple places, requiring pins, stitches, the whole works. Due to the loss of blood, the doctor told them it was best for Todd to stay overnight, but possibly longer if he did not recover fast enough. The police tried being patient waiting to talk with Todd about where he had gone, and more importantly, why he'd returned covered in blood. But they would need to wait—Todd had been sleeping for hours.

A sense of urgency had hit Howie after getting home from the hospital, while he tossed and turned in bed. He needed to talk with Cory and Ryan, as well as Mr. B, to let them know what Todd told him. It was clear their problems were only beginning.

He walked through the double doors of the school entrance, weaving in and out of kids clogging the hallway. Howie walked in a trance, looking for Cory and Ryan. Up ahead, he saw the principal and a few teachers standing outside of Mr. B's room talking. They did not look happy, whatever they discussed. The principal, Mr. White—a name which seemed fitting given his look—led the conversation. He stood well over six feet tall with a white beard in the Abe Lincoln mold, no mustache, and a balding head. The other teachers looked frustrated with the discussion. Mr. White waved his arms around while raising his voice. Howie intentionally slowed down as he got close to hear what they conversed about.

"Can you believe the nerve of this guy? Leaves a letter on my desk saying he resigned and wouldn't be returning. That's it! And he didn't even have the guts to hand it to me in person, he left it last night after everyone left," Mr. White snapped.

Before he could continue his rant, Mr. White noticed Howie listening to the conversation and stopped. He cleared his throat.

"Howie, what can I do for you?"

"Nu-nothing. Is Mr. B really gone for good?"

"It appears that way, son. Now get to homeroom before you're late, have a good day," he said, waving Howie on down the hallway. The conversation faded as Howie walked away, but he heard Mr. White saying something about how he'd never wanted to hire the weirdo in the first place.

Howie felt sick to his stomach. Mr. B was the only one who could help them with the evil entity that Todd had set free. And now he'd apparently skipped town, just like that. None of it made any sense to him. Just last night, Mr. B acted dead set on going out to the grave site and making sure nothing bad had happened. Did Todd know something he was not telling them? When he got home from school, he would ask his mom if they could go visit Todd at the hospital, try to get him alone so he would talk more.

Because he had taken the extra time to listen to the teachers chatting, it was too late to try and catch up with Cory and Ryan to fill them in. He would need to wait until film class. With a teacher workshop day on Thursday, and the big event on Friday, the kids had a rare five-day weekend, so the teachers thought it would be fun to do movie day during lunch. Normally the thought of that would excite Howie, but all he could focus on was getting to the bottom of this. It felt like they were racing against time and failing miserably.

✝

As advertised, Mr. B was not in class when they arrived. In his place was a substitute Howie had never seen before. The guy looked like he was fresh out of high school, only a few years older than the kids sitting in class. He sat at Mr. B's desk, distracted by a book he was reading when all the students piled in. The teacher looked up, annoyed he had to put the book down and do his job. He stood up and put his hands in his pockets, waiting until they all sat down. His hair was a shaggy red, hanging down in front of his eyes. Flipping his hair back out of the way, he counted the kids before handing out an attendance sheet to the first table.

"Okay kids. My name's Mr. Thomas. Don't waste my time, and I won't waste yours. As you've probably heard, Mr. B quit today, so for now I'll be taking over as your teacher until they find a full-time replacement. The good news? I don't care what you do with your time. So don't be stupid. The bad news? I don't know a damn thing about this equipment, so you are out of luck on using that."

Half the class groaned, upset they would not get to work on their films. The other half, the kids who only took the class for an easy A and wanted to coast by to begin with, were delighted by the news. Howie looked at his friends concerned.

"Guys, we have a real problem. What we saw in the woods, that was just the start of everything... Todd went back out there yesterday and freed her from the grave. He—"

Matt walked up behind them and smacked Howie on the shoulder, cutting off his sentence. "What's up, douche bags? Your little pickle puffer teacher couldn't handle this town anymore?"

Howie wanted to respond with a sarcastic remark, but right now he wanted Matt to leave them alone.

"I guess so. I'm sure that makes you happy, Matt."

"I'm pretty sure it makes the whole *town* happy. My dad will be thrilled with the news, he said nobody wanted him around anyway. Nobody besides you three at least. Wait a minute... Did Todd run off with him? Go rent a cabin in Vermont together?" He laughed at his own joke. "Whatever, you guys are boring. Have fun with ginger nuts teaching you the rest of the year. Not sure he will let you film your little pornos like Mr. B did."

Howie could feel his face getting hot. If Matt did not leave soon, he was going to snap.

"Why don't you go sit over there and try to figure out your second-grade math work while we actually take this class seriously?" Howie asked.

"What'd you say, you little shit? That mouth is going to get you in trouble one of these days."

Matt squeezed the top of Howie's shoulder, making

Howie's eyes water. He started to squeeze harder when Mr. Thomas walked up.

"Is there a problem here? I said don't do anything stupid and I'd leave you alone. Why don't you go sit back down, big guy?" he said to Matt.

"Oh, look here, a substitute who thinks he's got muscles. What do you make, like five grand a year?"

Mr. Thomas looked irritated, but he kept his cool. He stared at Matt for an uncomfortable moment. "Do you even know how many zeros there are in five thousand? My guess is no."

Matt turned red, his fists clenching at his sides. Ryan laughed, getting Matt's attention.

"Yeah, laugh it up fat boy. You'll get what is coming to you. Have fun playing make believe teacher, red rocket."

"Honestly, I'd send you to the office, but I don't feel like filling out the paperwork that comes with giving you detention. You're not worth my time," Mr. Thomas said as he walked back to his desk shaking his head.

Howie could see how nervous Ryan was after Matt singled him out. Ryan was looking straight ahead, trying to avoid eye contact with Matt as he hovered around the desk like a dog waiting for table scraps from the dinner table. Matt looked down at them and started to walk back to his seat.

"There will be a time where you losers regret what just happened. Watch your backs," he said, and then he was gone.

Looking around to make sure nobody else was listening, Howie told them everything he knew. He told them about Todd and his broken arm. He told them about Todd going back to the grave site. They agreed the next step would be going to visit Mr. B to see what he'd found out in the woods, and why he'd apparently given up his job at the school.

CHAPTER SIXTEEN

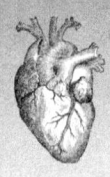

Cory walked into the local movie store; the big blue sign saying VideoSmith lit up the sidewalk. Normally, a trip to the video store before a long weekend would have him jumping for joy. But in truth, he had been on edge ever since the forest. He hid the fear from his friends, but he had not got a good night's sleep in days. By default, Cory felt he was the leader of the group. Maybe because he happened to be the oldest. Or maybe because he had all the coolest stuff and a take charge mentality. Either way, he felt showing any sign of weakness would be a bad thing. Cory felt grateful there were no classes the rest of the week. Ryan's birthday sleepover tomorrow would be the first chance the gang could actually talk about everything with no distractions.

This was more than a social visit to rent the week's newest releases. Old habits did not die easy, however, and he found himself stopping at the new release shelf. The first movie Cory spotted was *The Blair Witch Project. Oh hell no.* When the film came out in theaters, Cory and his friends snuck into the movie after buying tickets to see *The

Wild Wild West. Sneaking into R-rated movies was something they had come quite accustomed to over the last few years. The movie inspired them, giving them hope that a huge hit could be made on such a low budget. It helped direct them to the woods to shoot their own film. How ironic that they now were living in their own horror movie.

He headed toward the True Crime section, walking past the rest of the new releases. The real reason he had come was to rent the *Unsolved Mysteries* tape again. Cory thought it would be a good idea for them all to watch it together tomorrow night at Ryan's house. No stone could be left unturned. They still had no idea what they were dealing with. As he got to the row starting with the letter U, he heard footsteps approaching from the isle behind him on the beaten-up carpet.

"Yo, Cory. What's up man? What brings you in tonight?"

Cory turned around to see Lucas, one of the store's employees, staring back at him. He stood tall and lanky; tattoos ran from his wrists all the way up to his neck. Both his ears had large, gauged earrings. Lucas's eyes were a bloodshot red, likely because he'd smoked some weed before his shift. He looked high as a kite.

"Hey Lucas, I'm just here to grab something really quick and get home before it gets too late. Research for our movie, you know?"

"Hell yeah, can't wait to check out what you guys do next. You think whoever takes over will let you show it on access T.V. like old man Paul did?"

"No idea, guess we'll find out when the time comes," Cory said, agitated. He just wanted to hurry and get out of here. Lucas was nice enough, but Cory was not in the mood for chit chat.

"Okay, okay. Right on. Well, I see you're in a rush, so I'll let you get your shit and see you back at the register."

Cory was thankful Lucas got the hint. Hopefully his noticeable annoyance did not hurt their chances in the future of coming into the store and renting horror movies below age. Lucas had always been cool about letting them rent even though he was not supposed to. Looking out the window, Cory could see darkness already approaching the town. Rain appeared to be considering a visit as well as thick grey clouds were rolling in. Cory found the video he wanted and walked up to the register.

"Oh man, this one again? Haven't you guys seen this enough?" Lucas chuckled and shook his head.

"Can't ever do too much planning, am I right?"

"Sure thing dude. I'll be researching some shit with my lungs after work if you catch my drift." Lucas scanned the movie and took Cory's money. "I'll be hanging at my apartment tonight if you wanna stop by? Sweet mary J, pizza, and horror movies on the agenda."

"Nah man, thanks for the offer. My mom's been more uptight about me staying out late after what happened to Todd the other day. Enjoy your weed though," Cory said as he grabbed the movie and approached the exit.

"Always do, always do," Lucas said with a grin. He watched the exit door slam shut.

IN A SMALL TOWN LIKE NEWPORT, FINDING DEPENDABLE HELP WAS tough to come by. Especially with the low salary of a video store clerk. All Lucas cared about was getting movie rentals free of charge—the money was the icing on the cake. There was also the fact that he could sneak all the porn he wanted out of the back room and have it back in its place before the store opened the next morning.

Counting the cash in the register could wait until tomorrow; he had a date with Jamie Lee Curtis and his bong. Lucas turned off all the lights, set the alarm, and walked out into the night air. Rain had started to sprinkle down, bringing alive the distinct smell that comes with wet tar. He locked the door to the store and hopped in his beat-up Honda Civic. Reaching over to the passenger seat, he grabbed his CD case to find some tunes for the ride home. As he flipped through the sleeves, he settled on Significant Other by Limp Bizkit. He started the car, slid the CD into the player and cranked the song "Break Stuff" on repeat as he drove out of the parking lot.

The rain started to pick up, slicing through the beam of the streetlights. He squinted as he drove, the road a shiny and slick surface, making it hard to see the lines. *I really should have waited until I got home to smoke*, he thought. Lucas turned the wipers up full blast, hoping it would clear his visibility at least a few feet. He had never squeezed a steering wheel so tightly. The windshield started to fog up, only making matters worse.

"Oh, what the hell, stop breathing so hard, you dumbass."

Cranking up the defrost setting would be ideal. Unfortunately, his defroster busted months ago, one of the many joys of living by himself. Things that should be a priority took a back seat to the useless pleasures of his life. He didn't even make enough money to pay for all of his rent, but his parents chipped in to cover the difference, making sure their kid could survive on his own. He wiped away the steam from the windshield with his hand, temporarily clearing his view.

If the visibility was difficult in the main part of town, it only got worse as he got in the desolate area of Newport. His apartment resided on the third floor of a house that had been converted into three apartments, far out of town where rent remained dirt cheap. Right now, the other two apartments were vacant, leaving him in solitude, just the way he liked it. He turned down Breakneck Road, passing by the last streetlight as he drove onto the dirt road and into darkness. His headlights were now the only light available to him as the rain slammed on his hood, picking up intensity.

"I'm a mutha-fucking chainsaw, a fucking chainsaw," he sang to himself, trying to take his mind off the driving conditions. He felt as blind as his grandmother, picturing her sitting there trying to find what button to press on the remote to change the channel.

Lucas turned around the sharp corner, and something stood in the road up ahead. Not something. *Someone.* He slammed on his brakes, jerking the wheel to the right to avoid a collision. The figure stood hunched in the center of the road. His headlights lit up the silhouette as he fishtailed closer, revealing a set of glowing orange eyes staring back at him. The last thing he saw before his car lost control were the long, sharp claws protruding from its hands.

"Oh, shit!"

His car flew off the embankment, landing hard on its right-side tires. He tried to turn the wheel back to the left to no avail. The rear of his Honda slammed against a tree, the car whipped around and started to roll down the hill. Lucas felt a crack in his collarbone as the car crashed down on its roof. His head smacked off the steering wheel, blood instantly flowed from his nose. The car flipped twice more before landing upright at the bottom of the hill. A cloud of smoke forced itself out from under the hood. The music skipped before coming to a stop. His Honda sat in silence, the only sounds the rain hitting the car and the engine sizzling.

Lucas opened his eyes, his entire body hurting. His car now sat crunched up like an accordion. He was lucky to be alive. Looking around, he could see smoke filling the air around him. His collarbone had snapped; he had no doubt about it. The fear of other broken bones held him in place while he tried to grasp what had just happened. He thought back to the figure that he saw standing there, like it was waiting for an approaching car on the back roads. *What the fuck was that thing?*

It was hard to get to the seatbelt, the center console of the car was pressed up against it, holding it in place. Lucas tugged on the belt, trying to free it from the tight space. Finally, he was able to unbuckle, and felt relief as the tight strap slid off him. It hurt to lift his left arm, but he did it anyway to open the car door. He winced in pain, having to yank on the handle to get the door ajar. It creaked open partially before locking in place. With both his feet, Lucas kicked the door, sending it flying open. For a moment, he sat without moving.

He climbed out of the car and felt an extreme pinching sensation behind his knee. It intensified with every step he took, but he forced himself to continue. Out here in the woods, there were no houses for miles. Lucas needed to get himself medical treatment. Looking up the steep embankment, he knew climbing it would be impossible in his current condition. The rain continued to come down, soaking his clothes in a matter of seconds. He limped around to the back of the car, resting on the trunk. If he was going to have to walk through the woods, he wanted to grab his flashlight. The rain was freezing as it splashed off his exposed arms, sending gooseflesh all over his body. The trunk had slammed into the tree on the way down, but was surprisingly intact. Lucas yanked the trunk open and found the contents sprawled. His bong had shattered into pieces, something that upset him more than the car being totaled. He had been through so much with it, and just like that, it was gone.

"Rest easy, Bongkey Kong," he said, while making the sign of the cross on his chest. Carefully, he moved some of the shattered glass out of the way, looking for his flashlight. As he picked up a large, sharp piece, a noise from the other side of the car startled him. The glass cut his palm and he dropped it on the ground.

"Ah Christ!" He looked at his hand and saw blood coming out.

Again, he heard commotion up ahead even over the loud splashing of rain against the treetops. Lucas jerked his head up, looking over the front of the car, only to find nothing but the continuous rain. He held his position for a minute, listening for another sound.

Silence.

When he felt it must have just been the rain messing with his hearing, he returned to the trunk to continue looking for the flashlight. The light was tucked against the far end of the trunk in the back corner. Using his right arm to avoid the pain in his collarbone, Lucas leaned down into the trunk as far as he could, getting on his toes and stretching his arm toward the back. With his head in this far, it was completely dark, his body blocking any moonlight coming in. The car felt like it shifted slightly. He held still to listen—and heard the sound of thumping steps moving up over the hood. Quickly, Lucas tried to back out, smacking his head on the edge of the trunk.

"What the..."

Looking up at the roof of the car, the figure from the road stood over him, looking down with a predatory ferociousness. He was still trying to pull back when the thing jumped from the roof onto the trunk's lid, slamming it down on his bicep with a sickening pop.

"Oh, fuck!" Lucas screamed.

Her weight held the lid down, trapping him in place. He looked up at her as she crouched down close to his face. One look into her eyes, and Lucas knew he was living the last few minutes of his life. He flailed around wildly, trying to break free from the trunk. His foot kicked the broken piece of glass from his bong. If he could just live long enough to get ahold of it, maybe he could use it as a weapon.

"Please, the cops know I live on this road, they'll come looking for me when I don't show up at work tomorrow. Let me go... I won't say anything, I swear!"

He did not dare look down for the glass, afraid if he took his eyes off her, that would be the end of it. Inch by inch, he used his foot to slide it closer within reach. His broken collarbone sent needles of pain through his entire upper body with every movement. He crouched, still not taking his eyes off the woman, sneaking his arm down and grabbing the glass. Bongkey Kong had helped get him out of depression and saved his life. Maybe it would help him one last time.

She was still standing in a crouched position on the trunk, staring at him in silence. He could hear her struggling to breathe, sounding weak.

Lucas swung up with all the force his broken bone would allow him to and stabbed into her shoulder. She screamed, looking up at the night sky as rain poured down on her, the moonlight shining down on a set of jagged teeth. Lucas took advantage of the moment and pushed up the lid of the trunk, sending her rolling off the side of the car to the ground.

His arm had been impaled by the trunk latch. He pulled it free, the pain brutal. Attempting to make a run for it, the stabbing sensation behind his knee intensified, forcing him to stop and clutch the back of his leg. There was no way he could run with his leg busted up. He looked around and saw that the freak was back up and coming for him. There was nowhere to go. He did the only thing he could think of to get away from her and rolled under his car. All the injuries he had received in the past few minutes were amplified to an unbearable level.

This wasn't some horror movie where the victim hid from the killer, thinking they would not be spotted. He knew she'd seen him go under the car, and it was likely only a matter of time before she got to him. Still, the human drive to survive was strong. He pulled his arms and legs close to his body. Underneath the car, Lucas had roughly a one-foot line of vision out into the forest. He could see her approaching. Her skin looked disgusting; not the color of a healthy person. When she got close enough, he could see the mangled feet, the black nails curled over her toes. The rain peppered off the ground at the edge of the car, sending mud-splatter onto his arm and face. Her feet slid along the side inching closer—and stopped. For what felt like an eternity, she just stood in the same spot. *Maybe she didn't see me after all?* he thought foolishly.

Lucas attempted to hold his breath, but with the adrenaline pulsing through him, it was not easy. The bottom of the car sat only inches from his face, the smell of gasoline leaking out from the crash burning his nostrils. He looked up and a drop of gas plopped down into his eye. The stinging sensation that followed made all the other ailments feel like child's play. He bit down on his shirt to hold in the scream and curled his toes as he tried to blink out the poison. A soft moan escaped his throat, forcing

THE CURSED AMONG US

itself into existence. Lucas turned his head back to the side to see where she went.

She was gone.

That didn't make any sense. Why would she give up so easy? What did she want with him in the first place? Maybe she really was in pain, unable to continue her pursuit. It felt like wishful thinking, but he decided to cling to that hope. He kept his eyes focused on the side she had been standing, waiting to see if she came back. He would not get out until he was absolutely sure it was safe. His eye still felt like someone was scraping it with sandpaper. If he made it out of here, he thought there was a good chance he would lose sight in the eye.

He needed to control his breathing. He could not believe how loud he sounded. Again, he held his breath, listening for any noises. As he held, he could still hear heavy inhaling and exhaling. It took a second to register, but he realized it was not his own breathing he was hearing. Slowly, Lucas turned his head to look out the other side of the car-—and saw the orange eyes staring back at him, inches from his face. Lucas screamed and tried to slide away from her. She was crouched down low, army crawling toward him. The glow of her eyes revealed her facial features, but she remained mostly hidden in darkness, as though the shadows worked for her. He made it to the other side and started to pull himself out when she reached out and hooked her claws in the gauged hole of his ear. The force pulling on his earlobe was like a hook digging into a fish. So intense was the pain that he screamed out, the agony muffled by the pouring rain. She pulled him back under; he had no choice but to comply as he felt his earlobe torn apart. Whatever she was, she could not be human. She backed out, dragging him by one hand. The ear started to split as she pulled harder. When they were out into the open, rainwater ran down his face, making it impossible to see. Her hand came free, and she stood over his body as he watched on defenseless. She looked down at him and groaned, and then drove her hand with the force of a bus through his chest.

Lucas felt himself slipping away from consciousness. She ripped his skin apart and dug into his stomach. He started shaking uncontrollably.

"Pla... please, just kill me," he begged.

She pulled her arm free, looked down at him as the rain washed the blood away, and then gave him his wish, driving her claws into his skull.

CHAPTER SEVENTEEN

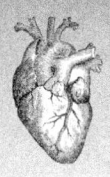

Todd tossed and turned in the hospital bed, trying to get comfortable. He thought he would be able to go home early in the morning after staying the night before, but the doctors wanted to keep him on IV fluids for at least another night. Not that he was complaining—the thought of going back to his house where that evil bitch had used him like a puppet made him queasy. She told him that he would be free after helping her, and so far, she had not been back in his head. Leaving the resignation letter on Mr. White's desk had been his idea, trying to cover his tracks. It took him three tries to get it right. The first time he got blood on the paper and flushed it down the toilet of the school. The second time, he felt it was too obvious a student had written it. That was when he decided to sneak into the library and type the letter up. He knew nobody would be left in the building besides maybe the janitor the kids called Razor Ray.

Razor Ray, formally known as Raymond, had worked as custodian at the school for the past fifteen years. Rumors spread around about what he kept under the bandanna he always tied across his forehead. Behind his tinted glasses, a set of bloodshot eyes always stared back at the kids, leading them to believe he stored LSD in the head piece, similar to what Jimmy Hendrix did back in the sixties. Ray always minded his own business, but if he saw a kid roaming around the school at night, Todd knew Ray would report it the next morning—that would have blown his cover.

There was a moment where he thought he might get caught, when Razor walked down the hallway whistling the song "Iron Man" as he mopped the floor. Todd hid around the corner, trying to think of an excuse as to why he was at the school well after hours with a bone sticking out of his arm and blood all over his clothes. Luckily for him, Razor turned down another hallway before he arrived where Todd hid. The broken arm had gone numb by this point as the shock well and truly set in, but he still had to type the letter with one hand. He knew his parents were already going to be worried about his whereabouts, so taking a few extra minutes to stop by the school before going home wouldn't hurt. Once the letter was in place, Todd grabbed his bag that he had thought to grab while exiting the woods, and walked his bike home—the sight of his mom crying in the doorway triggering all the emotions Todd buried deep inside him out in the woods.

As he lay in the dark hospital room, listening to the beeping of the machines hooked up to him, it all came back and hit him like a heavyweight uppercut to the jaw. He'd killed a man. And now he had also covered it up. Nobody would believe some monster took over his mind and made him do these things.

The moment he got out of the hospital, he wanted to talk with his friends and tell them everything he'd done. He knew they would believe him. It would be hardest to tell

Howie, who was much closer to Mr. B than the rest of them. Back at his house, he'd gotten so close to saying it...

These thoughts all roamed around his head uninterrupted when the familiar pain shot back into his head like a crack of thunder. *No, no, no!* Todd looked around for any sign of her. Through the door window, he could see nurses and doctors going about their business, wandering around with charts in their hands on their way to their next patient. He reached over to push the help button on his bed when she spoke to him.

Don't push it. That would be a grave mistake boy...

"You... you told me I was free if I let you go. Why are you back in my head? Go away!"

Be quiet! she boomed. *You will be of no use to me if they keep you locked up. Plans have changed. Your services are... still needed.*

"That's not fair. Please just go away, you've made me do enough," he cried.

I need more strength. I was gone far too long. I need to feed more...

"I'm not killing anyone else. Find someone different for your dirty work," Todd said.

The ringing in his head vanished. He had the hopeful thought that, just maybe, she was going to leave him alone, but it felt too good to be true. Todd looked blankly out the window at the night sky from his bed. It had started raining ferociously outside, the water pelting off the window. The rain, along with the steady beeping noises coming from the machine next to his head, brought on a drowsy feeling. He closed his eyes and started to doze off, hoping to sleep away the headache.

When Todd opened his eyes, he was lying on the hospital bed still, but he no longer saw the familiar surroundings of his room. The bed sat in the middle of the forest, moonlight shining down on him like a lunar spotlight. Confused, he got out of the bed and started walking deeper into the dark woods. Branches cracked under his bare feet, but he did not feel a thing. He could have been walking on jagged glass and still wouldn't have noticed. To each side were rows of tightly spaced trees, intimately twisting together as only pure darkness poked through. His arm felt better, the pain had completely gone away. Todd looked down at his arm and screamed. He held the machete in his hand, and it was covered in blood. He tried to drop it on the forest floor, but his hand locked in place—wrapped around the weapon. An invisible force urged him to continue through the woods. It looked as if the trees parted in the middle, showing him there was only one true direction to head. The flat terrain he walked on came to an edge atop a hill. At once, he recognized where he stood and hesitantly looked down below. At the bottom of the drop off, the body of his film teacher lay motionless, staring up at the sky with a dead gaze. His chest was torn open, the insides ripped out and sprawled across the ground. Todd tried to turn back, but his body froze in place, forcing him to continue looking down at the body. Tears started to fall down his face, so he wiped them away with the back of his hand. When he looked down at his hand, it was blood, not tears that he saw. He shifted his gaze to the machete, his reflection staring back at him as the moonlight blasted down on the blade. What he saw looking back was the white, expressionless mask.

The red tears continued to trickle down. Movement at the bottom of the hill snapped him out of it.

Mr. B was no longer staring at the sky. Instead, his eyes locked directly on Todd. Unable to turn and run, Todd had no choice but to stare back down at him.

"Look what you did to me, you little shit! She won't ever

let you free, not until you look like me!" Mr. B said in a deep growl not fit for a human.

Finally able to move, Todd turned to run—and came face to face with her. It was the first time he had seen her in such detail—and it terrified him to his core. The eyes burned vivid orange hell into Todd's brain. Her face was a gray pigment, one that had not seen the sun in twenty years. Cuts and scratches lacerated her face, open wounds leaking rancid pus down her cheeks. Slowly, a smile spread across her face, revealing a set of jagged teeth, blood crusted on their surface, a dark crimson red. Todd tried to scream, but his throat closed up.

You are done when I say you are done...

Todd woke up screaming, breaking out in a sweat. Doctors and nurses rushed into the room; the machines were going crazy. He looked around for her frantically while the nurses attempted to hold him down, trying to calm him.

"Don't let her get me! Please, keep her away!"

The doctors gave each other a troubled look. He was oblivious to their concern—all he cared about was getting as far away from the monster as possible. One of the nurses stuck a needle in his arm to sedate him. As he fluttered in and out of consciousness, he glanced over to the window. She floated there, watching. Waiting. She tilted her head to the side like an animal intrigued by something it was unfamiliar with, and the last thing he saw before he passed out was her disgusting hand, nails caked in blood and dirt, as she lifted pieces of a bloody heart to her mouth.

CHAPTER EIGHTEEN

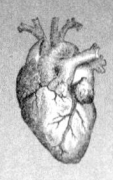

Ryan stared out the window, eagerly anticipating the arrival of his friends. The storm from the previous night had ended, and while the damage from the winds had knocked down branches and trees all over town, they appeared to have escaped any major issues. He woke up a few hours early out of pure excitement, even offering to help clean the house with his mom before they showed up. It was going to be tough to fit everything in that he wanted them to do. His mom had ordered the pizza a half hour ago, which meant it should be arriving anytime. As he watched for cars to approach, he could see his dad out on the lawn removing large tree limbs that had fallen in their yard. Even from this distance, he could see his dad's face turning red from the strain of moving such heavy pieces. With his dad's existing weight problems, Ryan wished he would not strain himself so much, it seemed dangerous for his health. It was a chilly, fall day, but his dad was still dripping sweat.

A car pulled around the corner and Ryan recognized it as the van belonging to Howie's mom. It was time to start his party.

"Mom, Howie's here!"

"Okay Hun, I'll be right there," she said from the kitchen.

Ryan had wanted everyone to arrive early in the day, but it was already almost dinner time. He ran out the door to greet his friend with a grin from ear to ear.

"Hey Howie! I got the Nintendo 64 all set up for some *GoldenEye*, wanna go play?"

Howie forced a smile as he got out of the van. He wanted nothing less than play a game that came out almost three years prior. "Sure man, is Cory here yet? I guess Todd can't make it since he's still in the hospital."

"Nope, you're the first one here!"

Ryan saw Howie flinch. He made a mental note to tone down his excitement, so he did not annoy them with his overbearing ways. Howie waved to his mom as she pulled out of the driveway, then glanced over at Ryan's dad.

"Hey Mr. Star, how's it going today?"

"Apparently I let one rip too hard last night and blew the branches right off the damn trees," he said and winked at Howie with a smile.

Howie laughed, but Ryan blushed with embarrassment. His dad always liked to try extra hard to make his friends laugh—and he set the bar pretty low by starting out the night with a fart joke. Ryan gave his dad a "please don't do this" look. His dad got the hint and nodded. He wiped sweat from his forehead and looked at his watch.

"Pizza should be here any time; why don't you boys go on inside and play some games before it gets here? We got cake, ice cream, and some good horror movies lined up tonight. Sound fun?"

Howie forced another smile and said, "Yeah Mr. Star, sounds great."

Howie picked up the gift his mom had bought and

wrapped for Ryan, and they went inside. The house was thick with the familiar smell of old bacon, as if they had just had breakfast a few hours ago. When they got into Ryan's room, it was evident that his mom put in overtime to make sure it was clean for the guests, as normally it was impossible to even move in the bedroom. Howie sat on the edge of the bed, looking around the room. The wall displayed a mix of old action and horror movie posters. In the corner of the room sat Ryan's desktop computer, something Howie could only dream of having. His parents did not have the kind of money for something like that. Not that Ryan's parents did either, but they did whatever they could to make Ryan happy—even if it meant having less elsewhere in life.

Howie had always felt a bit of envy of the relationship Ryan and his dad had. Perhaps that was the only thing he felt jealous about when it came to Ryan, but it was still always sitting there like a white elephant in the room. While Howie watched Mr. Star show nothing but love and care for his son, the relationship with his own dad left a lot to be desired. Howie wondered if that made him selfish. He had everything a kid could want—family vacations to Disney every year, amazing Christmas mornings, huge birthday parties, and he always had food on the table. But the one thing that he did not have was a close connection with the father figure in his life. His dad was not the type of guy to show any emotion—besides anger—toward his own kid. Howie always found himself trying to impress his dad, always trying to get his attention. When he saw how close Ryan and his dad were, it left a bitter taste in his mouth. Maybe that was why he was always pushing Ryan away. Why else would he resent a kid that wanted to hang out and have fun all the time? He always told himself to be nicer to Ryan, to not let himself get so annoyed. For whatever reason, he found it impossible to hold himself to that pledge.

"Cory's here!" Ryan's mom yelled to them.

"Nice!" Ryan exclaimed.

Howie felt a sense of relief—it was far easier to hold conversations when it was the three of them together. Cory walked into the room and dropped his backpack on the floor. His face looked like that of a kid who had put the first layer of zombie make-up on for a Halloween costume. Dark circles settled in below his bloodshot eyes, looking like Lucas after an all-night weed marathon.

"What on earth happened to you?" Howie asked.

"We need to talk like right now about what is going on guys. We keep saying we have to do something and then wait for more bad shit to happen. Why the hell are we still keeping this from our parents? I know you're worried about your dad's reaction Howie but come on man! This feels much worse than that."

Ryan cleared his throat and looked off to the side, mumbling "Yeah, about that. I... I mentioned something to my mom, and she told my dad."

Howie jumped up off the bed, his short temper getting the best of him. "What? We had a deal, Ryan! Maybe you guys wouldn't get in trouble if your parents found out, but you know I'll be screwed if mine find out."

"Yeah... well I think we're past the point of worrying about missing some stupid Halloween party, Howie," Ryan said.

Howie closed his eyes and sighed.

"It's... not just that, I wouldn't expect *you* to get it, Ryan," Howie said, glaring at Cory. Maybe Ryan wouldn't understand, but Cory knew damn well what Howie got put through every day of his life. "Well, it's too late now anyway... what did they say?"

Ryan looked out into the kitchen, making sure his mom could not hear them talking, and then lowered his voice again. "They promised not to say anything to your parents, if that's what you mean."

Shaking his head, Howie said "No, that's not what I mean. Like, what do they think we should do about it?"

"My dad seemed upset and basically told me to drop it, and not go back in those woods," Ryan shrugged.

They all sat in silence, digesting the new bit of information. Cory bent over and picked up his backpack, unzipped it, and pulled out the VHS tape.

"The first thing we need to do is watch this again. Think about it, the last time we watched it, we had no idea about any of the stuff we've come across the last few days. We could find some clues by watching again."

"Okay, once my parents are in bed, we can watch it in here. I don't want them to hear it though. I promised I would drop it when my dad asked," Ryan said.

"The next thing we need to do is go visit Mr. B tomorrow before the Halloween Homecoming. It doesn't make sense that he up and left without getting back to us," Howie said as he paced the room.

Cory thought about it for a second, and then said, "We can tell our parents we're meeting up to go to the party together. Think you could swing that with your dad, Howie?"

Looking uncertain, Howie said, "I think so. As long as I don't breathe wrong, or say something he doesn't like, or just exist," he said, trying to hold his emotions in check. "I'll make sure it happens."

Having a plan in place made them all feel better. It might not have been the best plan, but it was all they could come up with. Ideally, Howie would have liked to talk with Todd sooner, as he still had more information that he had not told them. One thing Mr. B had said to them was that the longer they waited, the stronger she would get. He thought if they waited too long, she would seek revenge on the town and not stop until everyone was out of her way.

As the pizza arrived, they left Ryan's room uncertain of their future, but for the first time in a few days, they had hope.

***

It felt like they were going through the motions of the birthday party. Ryan's dad cracked his typical jokes, and as usual, Ryan got easily embarrassed. After dinner, they all sang happy birthday to Ryan, and he looked like a little kid at Christmas with all the attention centered on him for once. Seeing it made Howie realize how truly important they all were to Ryan. In that moment, it was easy to see the good in him, and ignore all the annoying, attention seeking moments they dealt with. The pizza provided more than enough food, but they could not say no to cake and ice cream. After dessert, they all watched Ryan open his gifts. The pure joy on his face the entire time let them forget about the misery of the past week.

"Open the last present from me, son," Mr. Star said.

Ryan ripped open a tube-shaped gift, finding a rolled-up poster. He unrolled it, and his reaction was priceless. Howie could not see the front of it yet, but Ryan's face turning a bright red said it all.

"Dad, what the hell?" he asked mortified.

"Go on now, show it to your friends," he said as he burst out laughing.

Ryan turned the poster around to reveal a picture of Pamela Anderson in a soaking wet bikini, her back arched and water poured over her body. Everyone burst out laughing—everyone besides Ryan. He sat there shaking his head as they all cackled at his expense. His dad felt the need to twist the knife just a little more.

"Look at those nipples, Ryan. You could hang a bucket off those things!"

"Jesus, Dad!"

Ryan slammed the poster down and got up, storming off toward his room. Slowly, the laughing came to a stop. Ryan came stomping back into the kitchen, looked at everyone, and muttered, "Fuck off," while swiping the poster up and walking back to his room. This led to another bout of laughter.

"Thank you for that, Mr. Star, we all needed it," Howie said.

"My pleasure boys... speaking of pleasure, you better knock before you go back in Ryan's room, he grabbed that poster pretty aggressively," he said and slapped his knee in laughter, which converted into a nasty cough.

Howie and Cory got up and went back into Ryan's room. Ryan sat at his computer, looking straight ahead pretending he didn't care. He was visibly upset. Howie felt guilty at how funny it all seemed when it distressed Ryan this much.

"Oh, come on, man. Your dad's a riot, don't you get that? Stop making such a big deal about it," Howie said.

Cory looked down at the poster lying on the bed and chuckled again.

"And let's be honest: you absolutely could hang a bucket on those nipples."

Ryan grabbed the hacky sack sitting on his desk and chucked it at Cory. A small grin started to crack through the anger.

"Shut up, Cory. One pervert in this house is enough. My

dad can't keep it in his verbal pants for more than a few minutes at a time."

"Like we're any different! Be thankful your dad will joke about that stuff with you. My dad wouldn't know what to do if I brought boobs up in front of him," Howie said.

"Yeah, I guess I have to look at it that way. Just always feels weird when he does it with my friends." Ryan got up from his desk and walked over to the Nintendo 64. "Okay, who's ready to get their ass smoked at the hands of Oddjob?"

"Oh, fuck that! You know that's like a cheat code on One Shot Kill mode," Cory snapped.

"Birthday boy gets to be whoever he wants, Cory. It's only fair," Howie stated.

"Eh, whatever. I'll still take you both down. Let's do it."

And like that, they felt like kids again. A party they'd dreaded going to ended up being exactly what was needed to feel some normalcy in life. Time passed and before they knew it bedtime approached. Ryan's mom told them it was okay if they stayed up late, but given the lack of sleep they'd had this week, they all struggled to keep their eyes open.

"Oh man, we need to watch the video before bed. It's our only chance to watch it together before the homecoming tomorrow," Cory said with his eyes half shut.

He tossed the controller on the bed and popped the VHS into Ryan's VCR. He was about to hit play when Ryan held up his hand to stop him.

"Let me make sure my parents are in bed first."

Walking out of his room, he cracked his parent's door open, the un-oiled hinges creaked. They both laid in bed, his mom reading a book with her lamp on, his dad watching something on the television.

"Good night, thanks for letting me have the guys over. I appreciate it."

His dad looked up from the show and smiled. "You're our world kid. Anything we can do to make you happy. Best friends for life?"

"Best friends for life, Dad," Ryan said with a smile. "Love you guys, good night."

"Goodnight, Superstar," his mom said.

The only people Ryan was okay with calling him Superstar were his parents. It didn't take long for the name Orion's Belt to catch on. With the last name Star, and the first name Ryan, the bullies easily came up with the mean nickname, meant to say he was as big as a constellation. Just another thing about him for people to make fun of. But his parents meant well. On the happiest night he recalled having in weeks, he shut his parent's door and walked back into see Cory holding a notepad, Howie sat next to him, only the television screen lighting the room.

"Wow, look at you. Coming prepared for this, huh?" Ryan asked.

"It is legit our only chance, let's do this." Cory hit play, and the familiar creepy theme song of *Unsolved Mysteries* started up.

"*In 1978, deep in the forest of Newport, New Hampshire, a body was located, savagely torn apart. In the proceeding days, the trend continued as six other bodies were discovered in the same condition—all hidden deep in the woods. Police determined they had a serial killer on their hands, and went to work talking with the citizens, leaving no stone unturned. They were coming up empty handed—until they talked to the neighbor of Henry and Jessica Black. Barry Carl went to authorities reporting strange occurrences in the house next door, even going as far as claiming Henry was going into his house at odd times of the night. When authorities tried to interview his wife, Henry stated she was not well and could not talk. And with that, they had their suspect.*"

Cory paused the video and said, "We should talk with Mr. Carl too. How'd we not think of that? The guy had the best seat in the house to the shit show."

"Maybe because he's losing his mind? The football team doesn't call him Crazy Carl for nothing," Howie said.

"Yeah, you're probably right. And the less people we get involved right now the better," Cory responded.

They all agreed, and then continued watching the episode. Robert Stack did what he did best, setting the tone with his eerie voice. Up until this point, they were getting nowhere. And then it happened. An occult expert came on the screen, describing the symbols around the bodies. He held up a black stone, identical to the one Todd had moved in the woods. The expert was an older man who looked like he disguised his head with a gray wig, his face covered by a large, bushy white beard. He talked about the stones being obsidian and often used as a form of protection. Each body had some of the stones around them, indicating the killer believed he was protecting the bodies from something.

"Protect the bodies from *what*?" Cory asked.

It felt like important information to Howie, something they hadn't thought about before. Yes, Mr. B mentioned what the stones did, but why would Henry have put them around dead bodies? It also pretty much guaranteed the area they had found belonged to the body of Jessica Black. She was the only missing body from the reported murders; everything was starting to make sense.

The expert continued to talk about the stones, saying they would often be found in cases of possession and demonology. He briefly talked about how that would not defeat a demon but would prevent them from possessing another body. He said the only true way to defeat them is to burn them until there is nothing left, sending them back to where they came from, or performing an exorcism or banishment.

"Guys, this has to mean that's Jessica Black we found out there. It all adds up, and now that we know for sure, we need to talk with Mr. B. If what he thinks is true, we're in a lot of trouble," Howie said.

Ryan turned his television off with a frustrated slap to the power button. He looked at the clock—it was past midnight now; they were all about to turn into corpses if they did not hit the hay.

"Okay, we have our plan before the Halloween homecoming tomorrow, now let's go to bed, please?" Ryan asked.

They all hesitantly agreed and set up the sleeping bags on the floor. Ryan turned off his lamp and the room went dark. Tossing and turning, it felt like sleep would never come. As they lay in silence, only the sounds of Ryan's parents television could be heard through the wall. Howie heard a moaning sound coming from the room, listening a few more minutes before speaking.

"Um...Ryan? I think your parents are watching porn," he said as he started cracking up.

Cory burst out in laughter as well—the moans were undeniable now. Ryan jumped out of his bed, storming out of his room. He pushed his parent's door open, anger overcoming his foggy brain.

"Dad, what the fuck! You're disgusting. Turn that off!"

His dad fumbled for the remote, dropping it to the floor. Rolling over as quickly as he could, he grabbed it and turned the television off.

"How about knocking next time, Ryan?"

There was not much else that could be said when you got caught red-handed. He looked at Ryan, shook his head, and turned over in his bed to face the wall. His mom slept through it all, but Ryan felt like he had just been seen naked by the entire school. As if he did not have enough to get picked on for, this would take the prize. He walked back to his room, Cory and Howie were still laughing.

"Unbelievable," Ryan muttered to himself.

"Oh, relax man. Even dads need to spank it," Cory said, sending Howie into another spell of laughing.

"Shut up, ass," Ryan said chuckling.

Dead silence overtook the house. Only the sound of the clock ticking on Ryan's nightstand could be heard. Ryan felt his eyes getting heavy and did not fight the struggle to keep them open. After a great day, they all fell asleep.

Ryan awoke, unsure of how long he had been out. Cory and Howie were still asleep on the floor. The silence came to an end when Ryan heard sounds coming from his parent's room again. The moans sounded different this time, like they weren't coming from their television, it sounded like they were coming from his dad.

"For the love of god, this is ridiculous," Ryan whispered to himself, jumping back out of bed.

He almost tripped over Howie in the dark but regained his balance. Walking to his parent's door, he hesitated to open it this time. If it was in fact his dad moaning, what did that mean was going on behind the door? He heard his dad's voice but could not make out what he was saying. *So gross*, he thought. He took a deep breath, and opened the door again, ready to let his dad hear it. What he saw would haunt him for the rest of his life. His dad stood, facing the window in the pitch-black room. It looked as if he was in a trance. He was mumbling something to himself and pointing toward the window. With his other hand, he clutched his chest, then his body collapsed and hit the floor with a loud thud, the curtain coming down with him as he tried to hold himself up with it.

"Dad!"

Ryan ran to his dad as his mom jumped out of bed and came to her son's side. Kneeling, Ryan looked at his dad's face. His dad's eyes looked over Ryan's shoulder toward the window. His mouth was moving, but only gibberish was coming out. Heavy, labored breathing escaped his lungs.

"Mom, call 911, quick! I think he's having a heart attack."

She ran out the door in a matter of seconds, Ryan could hear the phone dialing the three digits nobody ever wanted to dial. His dad snapped him out of it by grabbing on to his shirt and pulling him close.

"She...is...*back*..."

A coughing fit cut him short. The labored breathing started to slow, until coming to a complete stop. Mr. Star died in his son's arms. Tears ran from Ryan's eyes; he started crying hysterically. He only faintly recognized that his friends were standing in the doorway watching it all transpire. Clutching his dad's lifeless body, Ryan was not ready to let the only man who had ever respected him go. It could not end this way, not when the last thing he said to his dad was calling him disgusting. His mom rushed in and got down, attempting CPR to no avail. Mr. Star was gone.

CHAPTER NINETEEN

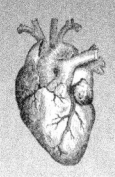

TODD GATHERED HIS BELONGINGS, HIS MOM AND DAD NERVOUSLY awaiting their son's departure from the doorway. Initially, Todd had wanted to stay here as long as possible. He felt safe surrounded by doctors, protected. But if the nightmare from last night was any indication, it didn't matter where he hid. She would find him. The doctors were not comfortable sending him home after the incident, which had led him to being sedated, but they needed to free up the room for other patients. While the freak-out disturbed the hospital staff on duty, the bottom line was that he remained a healthy teenage boy. They had no reason to keep him now that his fluids were at a normal level and his arm was in a cast.

"Hey kiddo, you ready to go home?" his mom asked.

"Yeah Mom, can we go to Country Kitchen for breakfast? I could use a good meal right now," he said with a grin.

"Anything you want, we're just happy to have you home bud," his dad said.

They left the hospital, walking out into the parking lot. It felt good to get some sunshine. He had only been there a few days, but it felt like he'd been trapped for weeks. The sun was starting to peer over the horizon, making for a beautiful morning sky. As they got in the car, Todd noticed his parents give each other a strange look—like they did not want to tell him something.

"What are you guys not saying?"

"The police... they want to talk with you later today bud. Nothing to be alarmed about, it's just that you showed up to the house after we called you in missing. They want to talk with you is all," Todd's dad said.

Todd shifted uncomfortably in his seat and looked out the window. He knew this moment needed to be dealt with. Maybe he should confess everything to them, get it off his chest?

Life had been far more enjoyable when his day consisted of annoying his teachers and making his fellow students laugh. Why did a teenager have to carry this much weight on their shoulders? It was apparent his life would never be the same, no matter how much he tried to distract himself.

"Yeah, we can get it over with I guess," he said.

"Are you sure? We can tell them you are not ready if you want to get settled back in at home?" his mom said in the softest mom tone she could muster.

"Yeah, then they can stop bugging us."

"Okay, then. Well first let's get you that breakfast we talked about," she said.

Todd could feel the eyes of the other customers locked on him as they sat at the table to eat. He tried to avoid eye contact with anyone, unsure of what they were saying about him. He knew some of it was in his head; it's not like his parents would be going around blabbering about him showing up at the house with a broken arm and blood all over his clothes. He also knew how boring Newport could be. Rumors spread fast. Some of the cops in town would be just as likely to spread gossip down at the Bowling Alley Bar when their shift got off. There wasn't much else to do in town besides bowl, drink, and gossip.

The waitress walked up with her notepad in hand and a smile on her face. She had the skin of a spray tan gone wrong and an orange name tag to match it. The name read PEG.

"What can I do for ya today?" she asked.

"Todd here will have his usual—chocolate chip pancakes with bacon. Orange juice to drink. We'll take coffee, thank you," his dad said.

He was thankful his dad ordered for him; he did not feel like talking with anyone. Looking around, Todd realized nobody was paying any attention to him like he first thought. *Calm yourself down*, he thought. Peg brought back their drinks and set them on the table. She crouched down beside the table, looking around to make sure nobody else heard.

"Did you guys hear about that Lucas kid who works down at VideoSmith?" she asked in a discrete voice.

"No, what happened? Did he get busted for selling pot to the high schoolers again?" his dad joked.

"No, I wish that was all. Police found his car all banged up in the woods off Breakneck Road. They think he lost control and flipped down over the banking."

Todd's mom held her hand to her mouth. "Oh goodness, is he okay?"

"That's the worst part. They found his body next to the car. All torn up," she said with a fascinated half-smile.

"They think he sat there a few days, animals got to the body before they did. He was all ripped apart." This time she put on a mock frown face.

Todd felt sick to his stomach. He knew there was no way animals got to Lucas. Evidently, the demon-bitch felt much stronger than she let on. It also meant she was getting closer to town. He felt like he wanted to throw up.

"I'll be right back, I need to use the bathroom," he said to whoever would listen.

He got up from the table, pushing past Peg and charging down the hallway. Todd opened the bathroom door and locked it shut behind him, staring into the mirror. Reaching down, he turned the sink on, taking handfuls of water and splashing his clammy face.

"Get your shit together, Todd," he said to his reflection.

If she was moving closer to the town, she neared full power. Did that mean she didn't need him anymore? Was he free? It was highly unlikely. If anything, he needed to worry about being her next victim. All he wanted to do right now was confess it all to his parents. Tell them the town is in danger, that she was coming for everyone. It didn't seem like a realistic solution. After what happened at the hospital, telling his parents about a demonic witch coming to kill off the town would only add fuel to the fire and get him sent to a padded room until he became a legal adult. What he needed to do was convince his parents to let him go to the Homecoming event tonight. If he could get together with his friends, there might be a chance they could take her down before it was too late.

Ignoring the other customers as he walked back out to his parents, Todd sat down and took a giant gulp of the ice water Peg had brought out. Thankfully, she'd gone to tell another customer her horrible stories. He looked at his parents, they were staring back at him from across the table.

"You okay?" his mom asked.

"Yeah, I forgot to use the bathroom before we left the hospital. I'd been holding it for hours."

He could tell they didn't believe him, but he also knew they wouldn't press the issue. He ate most of his meal in silence, outside of a comment here and there. Todd decided there was no better time to ask.

"I know I just got out of the hospital and all, but would you guys be okay if I went to the Homecoming thing tonight?" he looked down at his plate, afraid of what their answer would be.

"Do you think that's a good idea bud?" his dad asked.

"I feel like I've been locked up for so long. I really want to see my friends."

"Let's see how you feel later, okay? We'll play it by ear, deal?" his mom asked.

Todd gave a half smile. "Yeah, okay."

After they were done with breakfast, his dad paid the bill and they left. With everything he had been through, talking to the police no longer felt like a big deal. He wanted to get it over with. No matter how hard he tried, Todd could not stop thinking about doing whatever it took to stop Jessica. Even if it meant putting his own life on the line.

CHAPTER TWENTY

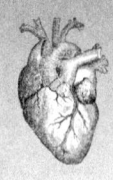

Ryan had always known his dad would not live a long life. He had always been severely overweight, did not exercise, and just did not take care of himself. Nevertheless, the feeling of not having him by his side still hadn't set in. All Ryan wanted to do was talk to his dad about everything going on. He sat on his bed, staring at nothing in particular on his wall. The only person who'd understood Ryan, who made him feel like he wasn't a nobody, was his dad. He could not bring himself to recollect the last thing he said to his dad. There had been no final embrace, no "I love you". The last thing he'd said to him was how disgusting he was —treating his dad like all the kids at school treated him. The haunting image of his dad's large figure collapsing to the floor, ripping the curtain down off the wall on the way down would forever be seared into his brain. Paramedics tried to revive his dad to no avail. They tried CPR before rushing him to the hospital, but they deemed him deceased on arrival.

Howie and Cory's parents came to pick them up around two in the morning. With everything Ryan had been through in the last twenty-hours, he still felt a sense of embarrassment at what happened. He wasn't sure if his friends would ever talk to him again. A wonderful day quickly turned into the most horrific night of his life, and his friends looked traumatized when they left. He also felt a bit of animosity towards them. While he sat at home to grieve by himself, they went on their merry way back to their families. Ryan would never get that feeling again. The thought brought him to tears once more—whatever tears remained after a night of crying.

Normally, he would turn to his mom for comfort. But she was handling it even worse than Ryan. His parents had shared such a close relationship they were always side by side. Now she sat on the couch covered in blankets, holding a box of tissues she flew through at a lightning speed.

Something Howie said to Ryan before he left had stuck with him. Howie had questioned what Mr. Star meant when he said she was "back". Ryan had not been able to wrap his head around it in the moment, but now that he'd had some time to think about it, Howie had a point. What could his dad have been talking about? He sounded like he *knew* Jessica, like he recognized her. When Ryan had looked to the window to see what his dad focused on, the yard was empty.

His parents told him they did not know the Black family. They said they avoided the situation altogether, trying to steer clear of town gossip. Still, something felt off. But who was Ryan to question their decision? He'd lied to his parents about the woods. He'd lied to his friends when he told his mom about going into the forest. The more he thought about Howie and Cory being more concerned with what his dad saw instead of the fact that his dad had dropped dead in front of him, the angrier Ryan became. All he'd ever been was a good friend to them. When they dealt with issues at home, he supported them. When a tough breakup crushed one of their hearts, Ryan would be there to try and cheer them up. So why did he do that for them when they clearly did not return the favor?

Whatever happened to the town sat at the bottom of his list right now. This town only made his life miserable; they could all fuck off for all he cared.

His mom sniffled and began crying again. One of them needed to break the cycle, so Ryan got up and walked out of his room to check on her.

"Hey Mom, anything I can do for you?"

She looked up at him. The face staring back at Ryan was one that looked as if it had aged ten years overnight. Her eyes were bloodshot, dark circles sunk into her cheeks.

"Oh Ryan, what are we going to do without him? I just keep thinking about all of the good times and it makes me so sad," she said and began crying again.

He felt his teeth digging into his bottom lip, trying to hold it together for his mom.

"He would have wanted us to remember the good times though. Remember the time he tried to mow the field out back too early in the spring? We told him not to do it yet, but he took the rider out there anyway." A smile slowly appeared on his face.

Waiting to see how his mom would respond, he paused. She blew her nose again, tossing the dirty tissue on the pile she constructed all morning. And then, she smiled.

"And then he got stuck out in the mud, splattering it all over himself. He was so pissed!" she continued. "The best part about that day, Ryan, was your reaction when he got off the mower and fell in the mud. I haven't seen you laugh that hard since."

They both sat there, laughing at the memory. The warmth the story brought them was exactly what they needed in that moment. It felt so good that they continued to share other memories for the next few hours. Laughing, crying, reminiscing. By the time they were done, his mom's tissue box was empty. Morning had turned to afternoon, and they were now starving.

"I think we should get Dad's favorite pizza for lunch and watch *Evil Dead*. What do you say kid?"

Ryan smiled. "Yeah, sounds perfect Mom."

It would eat at him if he didn't ask, so he changed the subject.

"So... Dad said something to me last night right before he... before he passed. When everything happened, he'd been looking out the window and pointing. That's what I walked into..." He cleared his throat. "And he was... talking to himself. When I walked over to him, he looked scared. He looked at me and said, 'she is back.' What was he talking about?"

He knew his mom could not have heard what his dad said to him, yet the look on her face told Ryan all he needed to know. They were not telling him something. She looked away, and at first, he thought maybe she didn't understand what he'd asked. It felt as if she was debating what to tell him. She grabbed a family photo off the coffee table and pulled it close. Looking up at the ceiling, she closed her eyes and whispered something to herself, before turning her attention back to Ryan.

"Superstar, there's so much I need to tell you. About this town, your dad, the murders... Please understand this was always for your own protection."

Ryan had no idea what she was talking about, but he felt like he'd been punched in the gut anyway.

"What do you mean Mom? What are you talking about?"

She took a deep breath. Another moment of silence

drove him crazy, he just wanted her to spit it out. Finally, she continued.

"Well, for starters, the murders didn't go down exactly the way the town says they did. And your father helped with the cover up."

CHAPTER TWENTY-ONE

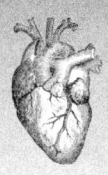

THE POLICE STATION WAS DEAD IN THE MIDDLE OF THE DAY. TODD sat with his parents in the waiting area for someone to come help. A plump old woman, her perm appearing two decades old, walked up to them.

"Why hello young man, you must be Todd, am I right?"

He nodded and waited for her to tell him what to do next. She pointed down the hall to an office. Behind the slightly stained glass sat Officer Miller. Todd saw him sipping a hot coffee while reading a newspaper; this made Todd feel a little better. Officer Miller did not carry the look of someone who intended to arrest a kid for murder today.

"Right this way, Officer Miller's ready to see you."

He got up and walked toward the office, his parents following behind. The lady gave a polite knock on the door before speaking.

"Officer Miller? Mr. Seymour's here to talk with you."

Looking up from the paper, Officer Miller put on a smile and sat his coffee down. He was an older police officer; his midsection told a story of one too many fast-food meals while on duty. Not that action came in ample supply in

Newport, but Todd doubted Officer Miller would be chasing too many criminals on foot these days. The police uniform stretched, trying to hold on to the buttons for dear life. Receding gray hair covered the top of his liver-spotted head. He wiped coffee off his bushy white mustache.

"Thanks Mary." He shifted his attention to Todd. "Hello, young man. Thank you for coming in today. I hope you're feeling a bit better after the accident?"

"Yes, as good as I can feel I suppose. Am I in trouble, mister?"

Miller chuckled and shook his head, sending a wave of relief through Todd.

"No, not at all. But in cases like these, any time there's a missing person's report filed we need to follow up. Make sure everything's okay, you know?"

Todd nodded, and Officer Miller continued.

"So, I got some questions to ask, just a formality, and we can get you on your way. Sound good?"

Todd nodded again; he decided the less he talked the better in a situation like this.

"Perfect. Now, we take missing persons reports very serious around here, but I understand what happened to you led to the delay in arriving home. First off, why'd you not go for help first? Why go all the way home with a shattered arm?"

He had tried to think through all the questions ahead of time, but he hated himself for not considering this one. The chair squeaked as he moved uncomfortably. His attention kept shifting back to the badge on Officer Miller's uniform. It let off a shine every time the cop moved in his chair, like a beacon of dread reminding Todd how serious the situation was. Something in the cop's eyes seemed off too. Todd didn't trust him, no matter how nice he was leading on to be.

"Well, I was so out of it, I just went where I knew to go. It really wasn't that smart now that I think of it."

Officer Miller chuckled again, tapping his fingers on his desk to an imaginary beat.

"You got that right kid. From what I hear, you had an awful lot of blood on you," he paused.

Todd sensed his breathing picking up as he struggled to control his emotions. A thought kept running around his head: the blood wasn't his and they knew it.

"That much blood loss coulda killed you. Doctors said there was more blood on your clothes than there had any right to be... for someone that was able to walk a few miles to get home."

Shit! Shit, shit, shit... The pauses Miller took after every sentence felt like a knife twisting in Todd's heart.

"So, where were you coming from anyway? Why leave your house when you were supposed to be home sick?"

This is something he had thought ahead to answer. He knew they would want to know where he had been all those hours.

"I know I should have told my parents I left—left them a note or something. Honestly, I thought I would only be gone for a quick ride. I'd been home for days, fresh air sounded great." He looked at his parents, giving them a look of sorrow. "And then, I just kept riding, I zoned out. The next thing I know, I'm flying down Fellow's Hill, and before I could regain control of my bike, I crashed."

"Damn, kid. You're lucky you didn't hit your head. I hear you had no helmet on either... That's a pretty busy road, how'd nobody stop to help you?"

Another question he did not plan for. *Real smart asshole. Way to prepare*, he thought.

"I wish I knew. Sure would've been easier on me if I got some help. All I know is I was glad to see my family when I got home," he said, focusing on his mom's reaction. She wiped away tears.

"Yes, I can imagine you would be. Listen, kid. I'm going to close this report and let it slide. But please, do not pull this stuff again. You leave the house, either get permission first or leave a note. Got it?"

"Yes, officer. It won't happen again."

Todd felt a huge weight off his shoulders. For now, he was in the clear on Mr. B's murder. Getting out of the seat, he walked over to his parents who were putting their jackets back on. As he approached the exit, Officer Miller spoke.

"One last thing. Something that's been eating at me this whole time. You said you were up at Fellow's Hill, one of the busiest roads in town, yet nobody saw you. When we went out looking for you, we asked everyone we chatted with if they had seen you out and about." He paused, locking eyes with Todd. "Only one person mentioned seeing a teen pushing his bike, but they said it was a kid leaving the cemetery," he said and smiled. "I probably shoulda mentioned that up front, huh?"

Todd's heart sank in his chest. This was it. He had to confess. The eyes of Officer Miller did not move, they remained locked on his face, waiting for a reaction. At his side, he sensed his parents also staring at him, waiting for a reply.

"I... I don't know who you talked to, but they must have remembered wrong. The cemetery is nowhere near my house, how could I possibly make it home on foot?" he asked, his throat was so dry, like a razor being scraped on the inside of his lungs.

"Hey, I'm only going by what I've been told kid. You wouldn't have happened to be out by those woods by any chance, would you? You know the town implemented some hefty fines for trespassing out there."

Before Todd could speak, his dad did it for him, and he did not sound happy about it.

"He told you the truth, Josh. He knows not to go out there and has no reason to lie about it. So, let's cut the bullshit and let the poor kid go home to rest."

An awkward silence filled the room. Todd felt like he could curl up on the floor and cry. All he wanted was for life to go back to the way it was. Jessica had not been in his head since the dream, but everything else had still been complete hell. He got the feeling his dad and Miller knew each other on a deeper level than just a civilian and policeman relationship.

"I'm on duty, Donnie. It's Officer Miller, don't you forget that. Maybe I'll make a trip up to the cemetery to take a look for myself, how's that sound Todd?"

Again, his dad spoke before Todd could.

"Do what you gotta do, *Officer Miller*. We're going home. Todd, Jody, let's go."

Todd did not argue, he walked out of the office, trying to hold in the scream that was trying to force its way out of his chest. It was only a matter of time before this all blew up in his face. He decided the time had come to tell his parents the truth.

CHAPTER TWENTY-TWO

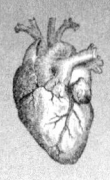

It took a bit of convincing, but Howie and Cory both finally persuaded their parents to let them go to the Halloween Homecoming. Not only that, but they also agreed to let Cory and Howie meet beforehand and hang out. Howie knew his dad hadn't let him do all this to be nice, he allowed it because it made his life easier. After Ryan's dad died in front of them, they had to call home and get picked up. Cory's mom handled it with care. She felt awful, showing her son compassion. She understood the weight of a kid seeing a man die in front of them. Howie's dad did not view it quite the same way. He was annoyed to be woken up at two in the morning, sending Howie's mom to go pick him up. Howie could tell his dad felt bad about it in the morning, but his short temper had got the best of him in the middle of the night. It was the first time Howie could ever remember seeing any sympathy from his dad.

Howie rode his bike toward Mr. B's house, the agreed upon location. They planned to confront their former teacher, ask him why he abandoned them, as well as get help in taking down whatever Jessica had turned into. Dusk was creeping into town, the streetlights flickering on as he sped down the side of the street. Up ahead, Howie could see Cory already sitting out front of Mr. B's driveway waiting. A beat-up old Buick sat in the driveway; a sign Mr. B should be home.

"Hey man, sorry. I got here as fast as I could," Howie said catching his breath after peddling up the hill.

"All good, at least he's here. He's probably been looking at me out the window the past ten minutes wondering why I'm sitting here," Cory said.

"Let's get this over with. Hopefully he'll have some answers. I don't like what we heard Mr. Star say. Like he recognized her or something," Howie said.

"How do you think Ryan's doing with it all?" Cory asked.

"I don't know. I feel bad we had to leave him, but if we don't end this, we'll all be joining his dad. Let's go."

The two of them walked up to the front door, only darkness showing on the other side of the windows. If he truly was home, it looked like he didn't want to be disturbed. Howie rang the doorbell, looking for any sort of movement from the inside. After thirty seconds, he pushed it again. Cory walked to one of the windows on the porch and peered in.

"I don't know, Howie. It looks pretty deserted to me in there. Maybe he's sleeping?"

"He's old, but not *that* old, come on. No way he's sleeping this early. It's hardly starting to get dark out."

After a few more minutes of ringing the doorbell, they decided to walk around the side of the house and peek in the windows. They walked quietly along the side of the house, crouching to avoid being seen by any neighbors. The sky was darkening, making it even more difficult to see inside. But it became evident nobody was home. Howie approached a window in the back corner of the house which could not be seen from the road. He pulled up on the latch and to his surprise it opened.

"What the hell are you doing Howie? I'm not prepared to break into a damn house," Cory whispered.

"He clearly isn't here, and his car's in the driveway. Something's wrong. And we know he went out to see the grave. We have to look," Howie said while climbing in through the window. "Let's be quick."

Cory stood hesitantly outside the window, shaking his head. He looked back toward the road, making sure nobody was around and climbed in behind Howie. A murky, cluttered room welcomed them, swallowing them in abnormal shadows and gloomy decor. Taking off his backpack, Howie searched for his flashlight and turned it on.

"Hello? Mr. B? It's Howie and Cory. Are you here?" Howie asked.

Cory punched him in the arm.

"Are you *trying* to get us in trouble? Way to announce our names to the world," he said.

They stood in place for a moment; nobody answered back. After they felt it was clear, Howie started to look around.

"Okay, we need to search for his research material. There must be an office or something in here that he keeps it in. Want to split up?"

"Um, fuck that. I don't have a light, and I sure as hell don't plan on giving myself a tour in the dark. This place creeps me out," Cory said.

He wasn't wrong. Something about this house felt very unsettling. And the darkness only intensified it. They walked down a long, narrow hallway, the beam of the flashlight exposing pictures on the wall with Mr. B smiling next to random actors and filmmakers. On any other day, these photos would have fascinated Howie and Cory. They dreamed to one day make films, and part of what drew them to Mr. B was knowing that he had worked in the industry before moving to Newport. Continuing down the hall, they approached a doorway on each side. Howie picked the door to the left, and they walked into what appeared to be the dining room. A large oval table sat in the center, cluttered with random supplies. It gave the impression of someone leaving in a hurry. Walking up to the table, Howie aimed the flashlight. A strange combination of black rocks—like those they found on the grave site—papers with strange designs drawn on them, and a map of the forest behind the cemetery lay scattered across the table.

"Well, this stuff is definitely something he planned to use out there. Think he never made it? Jetted out of town once he realized how bad it was?" Cory asked.

"Nah, his car is still here. If he left town for good it's not like he'd ride his bike," Howie said while picking up one of the papers holding the strange designs. "These are similar to the one we saw in the woods. He wrote sigils on the bottom. That's what that dude on the Unsolved Mysteries episode was talking about last night."

Cory nodded. "Well, Mr. B said something about protection stones that we disturbed. Maybe he was going to try and plant some new ones to keep her in the woods?"

They stood in silence, looking through the information, but none of it helped them. Howie dropped the paper to the table in frustration, looking around the room for anything else that would help.

"Let's look around the rest of the house, there must be more. He said he's been researching this for years, right? I doubt very much this is all he has to show for it," Howie said.

Cory sighed, hanging behind while Howie started to

walk to another room. Turning back, Howie held up his hands in confusion.

"What are you doing? We have to hurry," Howie whispered.

"We're in so far over our head, Howie. I know we agreed not to tell our parents because of how hard your dad would take it out on you, but shit man. We have no idea what we're doing! Why the hell do you think we should be the ones trying to take down some witch freak?"

Howie tensed up; the volume Cory was talking at felt far too loud.

"Honestly, if you want to go, I'll manage this. As scary as she is, my dad would make her seem like a puppy dog if he found out we went out there. He's been getting a lot more agitated lately when I bring up the woods, the murders, anything to do with the story really."

"Christ, Howie, I'm not gonna ditch you, especially with us this deep in this mess. But I still think telling the adults makes more sense than us trying to resolve this issue ourselves. Look what she did to Todd. He hasn't been right for a week and got a shattered fucking arm."

"I know you're probably right. But there's also the fact that Mr. B said telling the parents would be a bad idea. He came across pretty serious when he said that—"

"Yeah, and where's he now Howie? You need to stop taking everything he says as gospel. Just because he treated you nicer than your dad doesn't mean you have to follow his orders..." Cory stopped, realizing he'd crossed a line.

Howie winced, taken back by his best friend's hurtful remarks. His eyes started to water. Luckily for him, it was too dark for Cory to see. Maybe deep down he *was* chasing this monster to try and avoid his real-life problems. It was a hell of a lot easier to forget about your broken home when you had a witch coming to kill you. What would his dad really do to him if he found out they went out in the woods? Ground him? Being grounded had become a monthly routine. Hurt him? That happened just from putting something in the wrong spot. A beating would be like any other normal day. The realization set in he was being selfish about all of it, that he'd forced his friends to go along with this giant secret to avoid facing his dad's wrath and what he would do. It wasn't their problem, and now their lives were on the line all because they had Howie's back.

"I... I know you're right. But what can we do at this point?" Howie asked fighting back sobs. "If we don't stop her now, it's going to be too late. Mr. B told us she wouldn't stop until the whole town was dead."

"Let's keep looking," Cory said quickly, perhaps sensing Howie's distress. "There must be more than this that can help us."

Light continued to fade away as nightfall replaced the beautiful dusk sky. After looking in every room on the first level, they searched the upstairs. The biggest issue was they had no idea what they were looking for. All they knew was that Mr. B told them he had spent years researching the case, trying to uncover the true story as to what happened to Jessica Black. One thing remained perfectly clear—their teacher had not skipped town. His stuff was not only still here, but there wasn't so much as a suitcase pulled out, let alone packed. It all amplified the eerie feeling in the dark house. The sense that he had left with every intention to return home was evident.

Every room they searched came to nothing, leading to more questions than answers. Time was running out, and they needed to get to the Homecoming party soon. The last thing they wanted to do was show up empty handed. Mr. B said if Jessica got strong enough, she would almost certainly show her face at a secluded crowd to pick them off one by one. He made a point to say it was all an educated guess, but it was far more than anything Howie and Cory had come up with. As they walked back down the stairs and into the kitchen, only one door remained—the basement.

"Oh, hell no," Cory said.

"Come on, stop being a wuss. It's not like anything down there can be worse than what we are getting ourselves into out *there*," Howie said while pointing to the back door.

"Fuck me, yeah. Let's get this over with already. We better find something of use down there."

Howie opened the basement door to a loud creek. A black hole greeted them. It was odd how the house was modern, not an old clunker like half the town, yet the basement felt like something straight out of a haunted house movie. They walked down the unfinished stairs and were immediately hit with an old, musty smell. Flashing the light around, they could see the basement was partially finished. In the corner sat a long desk, bookshelves on either side of it jam-packed with textbooks. Howie walked quickly to the desk, Cory right behind. The beam of the flashlight settled on a stack of notebooks, a computer monitor, and a tape recorder.

"Let's see what's on this thing," Howie said and picked up the recorder. He hit the play button.

"Today is October 28th, 1999. I'm going out to the woods to find the location of the grave I believe belonged to Jessica Black. My concern is that I'm too late, that she's free and will soon kill everything in her sight. It's important to get my points across here, for anyone that may find this if I run into trouble."

Howie paused the tape.

"This is it man. I knew he went out there, so what's that tell us about his whereabouts?"

"Jesus, just hit play and let's keep listening," Cory whispered. "You're worse than Todd when we watch a sex scene. Pause, rewind, play. Over and over."

Howie shook his head and hit play.

"*From what the kids told me, the grave's hidden deep in the woods, and from their description it's protected by black obsidian stones and sigils. This gives me hope. If the protection is still in place, just maybe she's still there. I'm going to give a quick rundown of what I believe to be the case from my years of research. First, I don't think Henry Black was innocent. I believe he did in fact have a hand in the murders. But I don't think it was his fault. After discovering there was a Coven residing here in Newport, I dug into it. Apparently, they'd been around for over a hundred years in the area. They had a cult ritual to be initiated into the group. It's my belief that Jessica Black was a member of this Coven. That she practiced witchcraft. I think that eventually the group got in over their head. There are signs that they tried to summon a demon, and in doing so I believe the demon possessed Jessica's body. It's the only thing that explains the extra strength it would have taken to tear open a human chest with bare hands and remove the heart. The nature of the murders points to a demon like Atahsaia, the Cannibal demon. To trap a demon, a seal would need to be placed to lock it in. So, why would someone go out of their way to trap a demon in Jessica? And how did this demon go all these years without breaking free? Why'd Henry bury her instead of burn her body or perform an exorcism?*"

Howie paused the tape again, his body breaking out in chills.

"A fucking *cannibal demon*? Are you kidding me? I don't know if I can do this Cory," he said.

Cory did not raise his eyes from the tape recorder, staring back at it in a trance. He looked like he had seen a ghost.

"Hit play," he said in a terrified voice.

"I'm not sure how Henry overpowered the demon long enough to get his wife out in the woods. What I do know with almost certainty is that Jessica had control of Henry's mind. One of the things they practiced in the Coven was getting into the heads of the uninitiated. It would explain why all the victims' bodies were found deep in the woods when Jessica herself would not have been able to move them. I also believe that she had Henry kill for her when she was not at full strength. The victims did have his DNA on them, after all. So here's the thing... if this is all true, how do I defeat this evil entity before it's too late? Protection is of utmost importance. I will be sure to bring plenty of black obsidian stones, as well as protection sigils. It will be pointless to try and perform an exorcism, as Jessica's body is essentially just a host at this point—something else that doesn't make any sense considering a demon needs a living being to stay strong. Again, this points to some sort of seal keeping it in her body. My only thought is to try and take off the head, and burn it, but—"

The audio abruptly stopped, the recorder still played as if Mr. B had set down the device and not stopped it. Static filled the speaker, and then they heard movement as Mr. B came back.

"As you can imagine, I'm a bit on edge right now. I need to get out to the woods as soon as possible. I think if I destroy the body, it will send the demon packing. I'll bring salt to form a Devil's circle in hopes to trap it and pray that I can do this before it's too late. One last thing, I believe the Coven still exists today, that there are members in the town. I visited Henry in prison before he killed himself—yes, he killed himself, don't let the papers fool you saying otherwise. One of the last things he said to me was that she still resided inside his head from her grave, it drove him crazy. His bloodshot, crazed eyes still haunt me to this day. He said to be careful of the locals, that there was far more to this story than what had been told. The guard ended my visit

before I could get any more information from him... but it was a warning. This has coverup written all over it, and as soon as I take care of Jessica, I plan to expose the town. While Jessica did kill people, she was not at fault. Someone did this to her and I'll get to the bottom of it.."

The tape ended, sending the dark room into a disturbing silence. Neither of them knew what to say or do. It all felt so overwhelming, just a couple kids being thrown up against an evil entity much stronger than anything they could possibly defeat. Howie's eyes bugged out in excitement as something clicked in his head.

"Oh shit... Todd. He tried to tell us, he said she was in his head, that she made him do things. If Mr. B's right, she may have some sort of control over him, make him do stuff..."

"Like murder someone?" Cory said.

"Do you think Todd could have done something like that to Mr. B? They were both out there the same night," Howie said.

Cory stood at the edge of the table, letting out a big sigh and putting his hands on his head. He was not willing to move yet. Howie could tell something else had disturbed him.

"What is it?"

"What about this Coven thing he talked about? About how it's still around and that there is more to the story than just Jessica killing people? Do you think... like our parents, or teachers—the grownups of the town—are hiding something?" Cory asked.

"I don't know. All I know is none of that will matter unless we can stop her. Let's get to the school."

They climbed out of the basement, back toward the window they had entered to get in the house. Howie glanced into the dining room and made a quick return to the room. Opening his bag, he threw the stones and sigils into his bag. He ran to the kitchen as Cory followed. Frantically, he looked around the counter-space and found what he was looking for: salt. He threw the huge cylinder bottle of it in his bag and sealed it up.

"Do you even know what the hell you're doing with that stuff?" Cory asked.

"I know what a devil's star is from the Unsolved Mysteries episode showing us. If we can trap her in a spot, trick her to follow us, just maybe we can get rid of this thing."

He climbed out the window and waited for Cory to get out behind him. They got on their bikes and rode as fast as they could in the direction of the school.

CHAPTER TWENTY-THREE

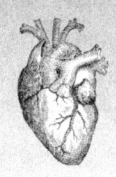

On the ride home, Todd told his parents he wanted to talk when they got back. He had some things to admit but wanted the ride to think about how to word it. Without any questioning, they agreed. The car ride quickly turned awkward with the silence. Todd's dad turned on the radio to his favorite country music station, something Todd would normally complain about. But in that moment, he welcomed it with open arms—anything to take the attention off him.

When they arrived at their house, sleep sounded amazing to Todd. They had been gone all day. The entire family shuffled in like a family of sloths. His parents slumped on the couch as Todd paced the living room and stood in front of them. The looks on their faces made this all the more difficult. It broke his heart to see how concerned they looked, how *scared*. He cleared his throat and decided he couldn't turn back now.

"So, I haven't been completely honest with you guys," he said.

They looked at their son uncomfortably but did not

interrupt. They were determined to let him finish before saying anything.

"Last weekend when I had a huge headache... that wasn't some random head cold. There's a reason it happened. We were filming our movie, and we went out in the woods behind the cemetery to get a few shots—"

"You what?" his dad asked angrily. "How many times have we told you that area is off limits Todd? What happ—"

"Let him finish, Donnie, let's hear his story," Todd's mom interrupted.

Todd made sure his dad would comply, and then continued.

"We went out in the woods, and while filming a chase scene, Howie tripped over something. We all checked it out, it was some sort of weird grave. Not one like in the cemetery, but like a mound of dirt with strange designs and rocks all over it." He looked to see if they gave any reaction, any indication of prior knowledge, but if anything, they looked as if their jaws were going to smack off the coffee table in front of them. "Well, I tried to be funny, and removed something from the grave. When I did it, I felt like this bolt of electricity shoot through my body. I started hearing this voice in my head, telling me to do all these awful things to people..." Todd started crying, unable to get his words out.

His mom stood up and walked over to hug him. He was thankful that she didn't try prying info out of him. In that moment, she was a mom trying to console her child. When she felt he had calmed down enough, she sat back down and let him continue.

"I... I did something really bad. That night I came home with my broken arm, that wasn't all my blood on me..." he said, feeling his body start to shake.

Sitting on the edge of the couch like he was watching a

close football game about to go to overtime, Todd's dad looked on, his jaw hanging slack waiting on his son's next words.

"I... I killed Mr. B."

His mom covered her mouth and cried out. Now it was her turn to cry.

"What the fuck, Todd!" his dad yelled. "What happened? How... why would you do that?"

Todd didn't get a chance to answer. Before he could get a word out, Jessica's voice came stabbing into his temples.

Kill them, kill them NOW...

He dropped to his knees, holding onto the side of his head.

"Noooo!"

As badly as she had hurt him before, this time was far worse than anything he had experienced. She felt stronger, angrier. He felt something pop in his head, like a bomb going off. The pressure mounted with an unbearable intensity. What felt like a warm fluid leaking through his brain slowly expanded, like a poison. When he lifted his head to look at his parents, his mom screamed at the top of her lungs. His eyes had gone bloodshot red, popped blood vessels making him look like a rabid dog about to attack an innocent kitten.

"Todd, what's happening?" his mom screamed.

She stood and tried to walk toward him, to comfort him; his dad still sat in the same position, seemingly unable to move. As she approached her son, he made eye contact with her. Behind his crazed look, she could see fear.

"Mom... *run*."

She looked at him confused, and that extra second of hesitation cost her. Todd grabbed a fork sitting on the coffee table and stabbed it up into her eye, the prongs wedging into the brown of her bulging iris. His mom backed up, reaching for the fork end sticking out. Her feet began to wobble, and she staggered, about to fall back. She gurgled an incoherent sentence and slammed down through the glass coffee table, glass shards flying across the floor. Todd looked at his dad, who for the first time since his son had started talking jumped up off the couch. He looked down at his dead wife, then back to his crazed son. Todd walked toward him, and Donnie began to back away toward the front door. He held out his hand, as if trying to tell his son to come to him, to escape this psychotic state.

"Todd... I'm so sorry. We didn't mean to do it to her. We tried to keep you guys safe, away from the grave."

As he backed away, Donnie reached blindly behind him with one hand, expecting to find the front door any second and make a run for it. Todd froze.

"Dad..."

Donnie felt for the doorknob behind him, but the door was not there. Instead, an opening greeted him with empty space. And then his fingers touched a person. He slowly turned around. The front door yawned open and standing in the entryway was Jessica.

She looked different than Donnie remembered. When they had performed the summoning, she had been a beautiful woman. Crazy, but beautiful. The girl standing in front of him right now looked like a monster. Her orange eyes felt as if they were burning the skin off his face. Her mouth opened to expose a set of long, razor-sharp teeth. Teeth that looked more like something that belonged to a shark than a human body. Donnie turned to run to the kitchen and only made it a few feet before something shot through his stomach. He looked down to see a set of jagged, talon-like fingers protruding through his shirt. He coughed blood, spitting it all over the floor. A brief thought that the blood might stain the rug entered his mind, but it vanished when

Jessica hooked her claws and tore upwards, ripping a hole from his stomach to the top of his chest. Donnie cried out and folded over on the floor as his intestines sprawled out below. He looked back at his son, hoping for one last look of sympathy before he died, but what he saw was Todd smiling. Whatever she had done to his son snapped something inside his mind. Donnie fell face first onto the floor, feeling his bowels release as he took his last breath.

CHAPTER TWENTY-FOUR

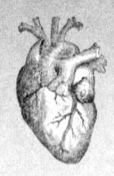

Howie and Cory peddled as fast as they could, the cold air burning their lungs. Up ahead, they could see the school and the glow of the bonfire around the side of the building. The parking lot already appeared full of cars, the party going strong. Howie hoped that people would arrive late so that they had time to prepare. Instead, they were greeted by close to a hundred students who all seemed to be having the time of their life around the fire. The Halloween costumes ranged from the Ghost Face, to Neo, to the South Park characters. The football team did not partake in something so childish, instead walking around with their jerseys on, like that was enough of a costume. Howie and Cory parked their bikes on the rack in front of the school entrance and ran inside. The school at least appeared deserted, with everyone outside enjoying the fire before the big rally and costume competition. The empty school building could easily have been a horror movie set; every step echoed down the hallway as their feet slapped off the tiles. Running as fast as they could, they rounded the corner. Howie ran right into Razor Ray, slamming kneecaps with him.

"Yo man, what's your problem?" Ray asked while holding his knee with a grimace.

"Ray! We need to get everybody to safety, something bad's about to happen. Please, gather everyone in the gym or cafeteria, somewhere safe!" Cory said.

Howie held his knee in pain, trying to shake off the feeling.

"What? Why would I do that kid? I just mopped those damn floors."

"Jesus, Razor! People are going to *die*! We need to get everyone inside and lock the doors, or tell them all they need to leave," Howie said.

"Hey! Stop calling me Razor, you know that gets kids put in detention. Take one look out there and tell me those kids will leave if I tell them to."

It was pointless, Howie realized. The eyes behind those shaded glasses looked as if they were enjoying a weekend trip to Woodstock. They would need to do it themselves.

They dodged past him and continued down the hall. Ray shook his head and continued pushing his mop bucket back toward the main entrance.

When they got in the gym, they looked out through the exit windows to where the bonfire blazed away. Cory glanced around for any signs of Jessica. So far, it was your typical small-town celebration. From here, they could see the stage erected behind the fire to host the evening ceremony. In the center sat a podium, where later in the evening Principal White would recognize all the sports teams and announce the best costume for the Halloween competition. Looking further down the stage, Officer Miller stood, monitoring the crowd. He had the look of someone who was waiting for trouble, not saying a word to any of the kids passing by. The fire raged on as the festivities were about to begin.

"Well, we can't get a boatload of people to listen to us, but maybe we can talk to Officer Miller, tell him to get everyone inside?" Cory said.

"No, after what the tape said about who might be involved, we really need to be careful about letting anyone know. But you're right, we can't get a ton of kids to listen to us, all we can do is try to get *her* to listen to us. We need to find a way to get her in a tight space so we can attempt the trap. Let's go before anyone sees us," Howie said.

Raymond stopped the mop bucket in front of the main office entrance. Looking up at the clock, he decided it was about time to clock out for the night. It was a bit depressing knowing that all the hard work he put in today would be destroyed tomorrow morning when he came back. These kids acted like savages, leaving shit all over the floor, knocking over trash cans, among many other inconveniences to Ray's day to day responsibilities. To top it off, they all treated him like some kind of burnout druggie. He heard all the stories going around about him. Some of them hurt, not only insulting his intelligence but his family. Kids could be vicious, and the town of Newport was no different. Sure, the teachers all acted friendly with him face to face. But he also knew when they sat in the break room and mingled with the other "intelligent" folks, they were no better than the kids. Nobody really knew his true backstory. That he had been a hero, saving a kid's life and suffering a life altering injury in the process.

Years ago, while out Christmas shopping in the city, Ray

came across a few bullies beating up a scrawny kid in a back alley. The kid fought for his life, getting bloodied to a pulp. To this day Ray was not sure why they did it, but in the moment none of that mattered. He acted fast, charging down the narrow dark opening and yelling at the bullies to stop. They looked up at him, telling him to get lost. For a moment, he considered it. Then the kid made eye contact with him from the ground, the fear in his eyes bringing back so many memories of Ray's childhood that he felt no choice but to intervene. He charged at the bullies, not sure what he planned to do—but knowing damn well he was going to stop them from any more beating. What he didn't realize was a third bully remained shrouded in darkness, coming from the side when he wasn't prepared for it. The impact of something hard struck the back of his head, sending him into a daze. That was all he recalled happening, but after he had been knocked out, they continued hitting him. When he awoke, he was in a hospital, his vision impaired by bruises and broken blood vessels. Something else was wrong too; he couldn't talk in coherent sentences. He later found out that there had been brain damage, affecting his motor skills. While some of his functions returned to normal—like walking and eating, many did not and never would come back.

So, did he do drugs? Yes. But he sure as hell did not do the drugs kids thought he did. The drugs he took helped him to survive, to ease the pain in his head he dealt with every day. If any of them ever took a minute to stop the insults and dig into his past, they would have seen he was not some hippie-stoner drug addict. They would see he was a hero, that he saved a kid's life who likely would have been beaten to death in a back alley.

Ray walked into the office with a bottle of Windex and paper towels. The room had huge windows that stretched from the ceiling all the way down to the center of the wall. They were a pain in the ass to clean, especially for a handicapped individual, but he did the best he could. He sprayed the pane as high as he could reach, watching the liquid sliding down the fingerprint-covered glass. On the other side of the window stood the main entrance to the school. Through the blur of the spray, he could see what looked like kids continuing to walk past the entrance toward the back of the school outside. Raising the bottle, he continued to spray across the entire bottom half of the window, letting it set in before he would wipe it away. He saw movement behind the blur of the cleaning product and realized a student must be coming in through the front entrance. *Stupid kids, a sign is right there telling them to go around the back,* he thought. Wiping away the spray, whoever had just walked in was no longer in his line of sight. He cleared it just in time to see the front door latch shut.

Most of the lights in the school were off to save energy. Ray sat the spray and the paper towels on Principal White's desk and walked back to the office door. There was nobody in the hallway that he could see. Maybe the kid read the sign after all and turned back outside?

"Hello? Hey kid, whoever came in this way, the sign tells you not to use the front door..."

Nobody responded to him. The hallways were deserted. The only sound was the squeaking of his shoe-tread on the glossy floor he had mopped only moments ago.

"Stupid little prick. I know someone came in, just get lost will ya?" He shook his head and returned to the office to finish cleaning.

The Windex had slid down the glass and settled at the bottom of the window frame. Irritated, Ray grabbed a paper towel and aggressively wiped it away. Moving down to the next window, he started the process again. As he reached

THE CURSED AMONG US

up to wipe, the lights in the office went out, sending him into complete darkness.

"That's it, I'm done playing nice," he muttered.

Slamming the cleaning bottled down on the table, he stormed out the door into the hallway, tripping over the mop bucket that he had left there on his way in. He landed on his hip, pain shooting down his leg. Water spread across the clean floor as a bright red exit light shone down onto the wet tiles. In the water's reflection, he saw the outline of a figure standing behind him and whipped his head around. Standing above him was a kid in a costume, looking down on him, confused. The kid had a white mask on; what looked like blood dripped down the eyes of a face that showed no expression whatsoever. In the kid's hand was a long machete, and Ray's first thought was that it looked far too real to be a costume prop.

"Is something wrong with you kid? Why you standing there? Go out the front door and around like the rest of the kids," Ray said, trying to sound tough.

The kid didn't budge. The long silence was starting to become disturbing. Ray stood up, holding his sore hip and wincing. He bent over, righted the mop bucket, and grabbed the mop from the floor. It was not something he would admit to this kid, but he was starting to get spooked. The red exit light illuminated the hallway, the kid standing in place as if he was waiting for something. Finally, the kid moved his head, tilting it slightly to look over Ray's shoulder. Ray felt his grip tighten on the mop handle, debating if he should make a run for it or show this kid he'd pranked the wrong guy. That's when something grabbed the back of his head with an inhuman strength and squeezed. He screamed, unable to move, unable to see who grabbed him. Willing his eyes to look down, Ray saw the ghastliest set of feet he had ever seen. Long, sharp black toenails stuck out from each toe. The skin was a grayish tone, soiled in dirt and blood. He tried to break free, but the strength of the fingers around his skull was far too great. It felt like his head was being held in place by a vice with someone slowly tightening its grip inch by inch.

"Help! Somebody, help me!" Ray screamed.

He tried again to break free, and once again was unsuccessful. The hand gripping his head pushed down, forcing his head toward the ground. The top of the mop handle was now only a few inches from his face, getting closer. A thought occurred to try and hit whoever stood behind him with the mop. The hand squeezed tighter, and he felt nails digging into the back of his skull; he imagined they matched what he saw on the feet, like bird talons. Ray opened his mouth to scream again when the hand drove his head down, the mop handle lodging into his open mouth and forcing its way out of the back of his head. Brain matter and blood escaped, gushing all over the floor, all over Jessica's feet.

Jessica Black looked at Todd, who she now had complete control over, his brain turned to mush now that she was at full strength.

Go, it is time they pay for what they have done to me.

Todd did as he was told. He couldn't have done anything different if he wanted to at this point, he felt like a prisoner in his own body, being controlled at will.

CHAPTER TWENTY-FIVE

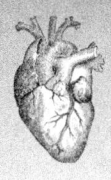

Ryan pulled into the school's parking lot, driving his dad's Jeep like one would expect of a kid that didn't possess a license. His mom had begged him to stay, but after she told him the story of his dad's past and how it tied to Jessica, he would stop at nothing to make sure the bitch was gone for good. In the back seat, he had brought the only weapon he had—his wooden bat. He slammed on the breaks and put the vehicle into park, opening the door before the jeep came to a complete stop and got out. Before he even got the bat from the back, he heard screams coming from around the backside of the school where the bonfire burned away. Quickly, he grabbed the weapon and sprinted in the direction of the chaos.

He spent a few hours earlier taking in what his mom told him. It crushed him inside. His friends abandoned him when he was at his weakest, which he could look past. It was nothing new for them to put everything else ahead of him—vulnerable, or not. What really tore him apart was learning that his dad had betrayed him all these years, only acting like he was looking out for Ryan. His entire life felt like a farce. A big, fat lie. It all seemed fitting.

His mother told him everything, until she started crying so hard, he couldn't make out any more of what she was saying. But he heard enough, enough to leave the house with her pleading for him to stay.

His dad had partaken in lying to the feds about the true killer. All these years, he knew her body was out there and told his son to stay away from the woods because of the murders, not because he was guilty of making sure she never got discovered. It went far beyond his dad too. Many members of the town—including some parents, teachers, cops—were in on the coverup. At first, Ryan could not grasp why an entire town could do such a thing. It felt impossible to have that many people keep a secret for so long. He asked his mom why they'd done it, why they went out of their way to lie to the feds, preventing them from going out to those woods to look for her. And what about all the murders? Part of him wished he never asked, but he did anyway, and she told him.

Ryan rounded the corner of the building and saw the huge bonfire raging in front of him. Kids were running in every direction; their expressions were those of pure terror. Some of them ran into the school through the gymnasium doors, others ran for the parking lot, trying to get in their cars and take off. One girl that he knew from his history class named Tabitha Baisley got into her car and started it up. She was so hysterical that she wasn't paying any attention to her surroundings. If she had been, she would have noticed the kids scrambling behind her, trying to get to their own vehicles. Ryan watched on in horror as she backed out and slammed into two girls running by. One of the girls avoided most of the contact, getting clipped by the passenger mirror as the car launched back. The other girl was not so lucky. A loud thump cut her screams short as the car backed up and over her, one of the tires crushed both her legs as it passed over—something that would have forced another scream out had it not been for the other tire popping her head like a zit spewing pus all over the bathroom mirror. Tabitha stopped the car and opened her door, when she realized what she'd done she cried out before shutting the door and backing the rest of the car over the body and speeding off down the road. Somehow, Ryan still felt she would end up being the fortunate one.

Bodies ran in every direction like scurrying ants about to get stomped on by a giant shoe. The source–what they were running from–had not yet identified itself, but Ryan already knew what the cause of the ensuing madness was. Jessica. Most of the football team were still up on the stage, unable to climb down with all the other kids running below and blocking the stairs. Mr. White stood at the podium, trying to regain control of the large crowd.

"Please, make your way into the school to safety! Form a single file line and wait until the kid in front of you is inside before trying to enter!" he said into the microphone.

His voice boomed over the loudspeakers they had set up earlier in the day, but he might as well have been whispering to himself. Students ran into each other, some falling and getting trampled while others pushed the weaker kids out of the way. The blazing fire blocked most of the stage, obscuring Ryan's view. He hoped that Cory and Howie somehow made it to safety if they had even arrived yet. Up on the stage, Matt was up to his usual bullying ways. By far the biggest kid on the team, he spent no time deciding if he wanted to help others or help himself. He pushed Coach Carl out of the way, and the old, fragile man fell to the ground. His combover hair came undone as he attempted to crawl out of the way of the team while they stomped over the top of him to get free. Matt jumped off the side of the stage and plowed through the crowds toward the school. Ryan turned his attention back to the stage, his heart almost bursting out of his chest.

Through the fire, through the crowd of crazed students, Jessica slowly rose above the flames. She soared a few inches over the stage, hovering above as she looked down upon her future prey with a gaze that sent gooseflesh across Ryan's body. For the first time, lit by the fire, he got a very clear picture of what she looked like. Her hair clung to her body in long, black strands with patches missing, streaks of dried blood spread throughout. The dress she wore had turned the color of mud and dried blood; rips scattered across the fabric in random spots. Her fingernails were long, sharp, and ink black. They reminded Ryan of talons you would see on a hawk, curled into a hook on each finger. He noticed blood dripping from her chin and looked down to see a body torn apart on the stage, its insides smeared across the platform. Panic set in as Ryan wondered who she'd killed. Could it be one of his friends? He walked around the side of the fire to get a closer look, avoiding the oncoming traffic of kids and teachers fleeing for their lives. Under the blood and body parts, he made out the team's football uniform.

Jessica arched her back and looked up at the night sky. Her arms stretched behind her back at an abnormal angle, and Ryan watched as her claws appeared to extend another few inches. She screamed louder than anything he had ever heard in his life. Some students continued filing into the school, others dropped, holding the sides of their heads as the volume was too much to handle. Ryan looked down at his weapon and realized how foolish he'd been for thinking a baseball bat could take down something like this. He remained determined to kill her, but right now, his best option was to regroup at the school and wait for a better opportunity to come. Instead of following the crowd, Ryan jogged back around the front of the building—something others picked up on as well. Kids sprinted past him yelling incoherently. For once, he was on their level. Nobody picked on him, nobody called him fat. There were far bigger concerns than the high school pecking order. He reached the school entrance and walked inside to an eruption of turmoil. While most kids gathered in the gym, he decided it best to go somewhere where he felt he had an advantage. He ran in the opposite direction to the others, formulating a plan in his head as he went.

CHAPTER TWENTY-SIX

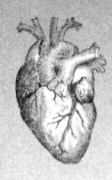

After searching the entire lower level of the school for a space to try and trap Jessica, Howie and Cory were running out of ideas. They considered setting up their trap in the film editing room as it was a tight space they could get her cornered in. The problem with that idea was that no other way out of the room existed. If she came in hot on their heels, they would be stuck. At least sitting in the film room gave them time to think things over more. All Howie wanted to do was end the nightmare, to make Mr. B proud and avenge his likely death. He had put his life on the line for the students, and now they could return the favor. Howie looked out through the door's window into the hallway; they remained alone for now.

"Well, I think this spot is still our best bet, Cory. We can try to bait her into coming in the studio and then lock her in. If I can get the star set up in here and she happens to go in, she won't be able to move."

"And then what, Howie? She sits in here and is forced to watch our shitty movies for eternity? What are we going to do with her?" Cory asked.

THE CURSED AMONG US

Howie opened the door and started to walk out of the soundproof room.

"We heard what Mr. B said on the tape, the way he thought she could be defeated. We just need—"

Screams and commotion erupted. From the soundproof editing studio, they hadn't been able to hear the sounds outside. *How long has that been going on out there?* Howie thought. The film room had an emergency exit out to the parking lot. Howie ran to the door and popped it open a few inches. The parking lot looked like a highway car wreck; multiple head on collisions by the exit, one car had t-boned another in the driver's side door. Any remaining students had either stayed behind to help those who had been hurt or happened to be the unfortunate ones who needed help. The fire continued undisturbed, the image of the blaze and kids lying hurt or worse—*dead*, presented a real-life Hell on Earth scene. There was no sign of Jessica anywhere, but she had left her mark.

"Holy hell, I think we're too late..." Howie said. He tossed his bag over his shoulder, and they quietly walked out into the night. As they came around the side of the stage, they saw Mr. Carl motionless, covered in blood. The gaze of his lifeless eyes staring back at them made Howie nauseous. A teacher who had just given them a lesson on *Beowulf* only a few days ago now lay dead at the hands of a monster.

Looking around now that they closed in on the scene, Mr. Carl was not the only casualty at the school celebration. It was a scene that would be chiseled into their brains forever. They made their way to the door of the gym and walked in. Kids sat sobbing on the platform behind the basketball hoop, checking each other's wounds. Mr. White and Officer Miller stood in the corner talking with one another, likely trying to come up with a plan. At the sight of Howie, Mr. White shifted his attention to them.

"Howie! Are you two the last to come in?"

Howie nodded, too shocked to do anything more than that.

"Quickly, lock the door! We need to block off the windows and stay in here until help can arrive!"

Reluctantly, Howie turned back and found the lock, latching it into place. He had wanted everyone in here, but he had no intention of being part of that equation. There would be no way to end this if they remained locked up with the rest of the crowd. When he turned back around, the reality really set in. He imagined this is what battlefields looked like during wars—some wounded, some crying, some on the floor either dead or unconscious. Cory walked over to Bethany, sitting on the floor with a few friends, visibly upset. Howie noticed him trying to comfort her and decided to wait a few minutes before walking over. Instead, he walked up to another kid he had never talked to before who was a few grades above Howie.

"What happened out there?" he asked, afraid to know the answer.

The kid shook his head in a daze. "Dude... some crazy flying chick came out of nowhere and started... eating people or something," he said.

"Where'd she go? Did you see which direction?"

"Hell no! I ran the opposite direction of that crazy shit. I hope I never see her again to be honest." He walked away before Howie could ask any more questions.

Everyone sat scattered across the gym. When he and Cory had snuck by the crowd earlier, there had been far more students and teachers than those now sheltered in here. Hopefully some got away, but the parking lot still looked mostly full of vehicles. It was more likely that more people lay helpless outside—or else dead.

He needed to find a way to get out of here so they could see their plan through. Howie walked over to Cory and Bethany.

"Hey Bethany, glad to see you made it back here..." He didn't know what else to say to her in the moment.

Cory looked up at him, concerned. "We have bigger issues than we thought, Howie. Bethany told me what happened out there. I just don't see how we can stop this by ourselves."

Bethany looked at Cory like he was crazy.

"Wait, what? You plan to try and stop her? Are you insane? This isn't one of your movies, she'll *kill you*."

"We have no choice. Mr. B was the only one who knew how to stop her, and he's... gone," Howie said.

"What exactly did you superheroes have in mind?" she asked.

"Mr. B said in order to trap her, we needed protection—which we have—and that we needed to get her in a secluded area so we could get her in a Devil's circle—" Cory said before she interrupted him.

"Devil's circle? Mr. B knew about this? I'm so confused."

"We don't have time to explain it all right now, but we will later. Bethany, can you please do us a favor and distract Mr. White and Officer Miller so we can sneak out of here?" Howie asked.

Bethany paused for a moment, looking around at all the students in pain, taking in all of the sadness.

"I... I guess. Please don't get yourselves killed, I kinda like you guys," she said.

Before they walked away, she walked up to Cory and kissed him on the cheek, and then she hurried on her way to talk to the adults.

"Man, if I die before I can sit down and enjoy the fact that the girl of my dreams just kissed me, I'm going to come back as a ghost and haunt the shit out of you," Cory said.

✞

The halls were deathly quiet compared to the gym and the bonfire. Howie and Cory sprinted down the hall looking for any sign of activity. The lights in the school had been turned off, the only light coming from the exit signs and spotlights in the stairwells. They approached the front office and found Razor Ray torn apart on the floor, his head stuck on the handle of his mop like some merciless trophy.

"Oh my god, I'm going to be sick," Cory said, and leaned against the wall, taking deep breaths.

"She might be close, let's be quiet..." Howie said, unable to take his eyes off the janitor.

As they passed Ray, they walked down the next hallway, the corridors filled with lockers shrouded in darkness. They stood for a moment, unsure which direction they wanted to go. Screaming from behind them caught their attention, and they both turned to see what was going on. Their art teacher, Mrs. Baxter, was running toward them, her dress covered in blood.

"Run! He's killing everyone!" she screamed.

"*He?*" Cory whispered.

Then they saw who she was talking about, and their worlds came crashing down. Todd stalked toward Mrs. Baxter, wearing his killer costume—machete and all. The blade was covered in blood, and Howie had the feeling it wasn't red syrup this time. Mrs. Baxter did not see the dead body of Ray on the ground in front of her, tripping over him as she let out another scream. Howie and Cory watched, still unsure of what their friend was going to do. Todd stood over her as she tried to back away, begging for her life. In one fast swipe, he sliced her throat with the blade, sending blood spraying in every direction.

"No!" Cory shouted.

Howie grabbed Cory by the sleeve and pulled him down the hallway. They took off in a sprint, unsure if Todd had seen them go in this direction. Taking a risk, Howie looked back into the dark hallway they had come from—and nobody followed. A decision needed to be made quick; it was only a matter of time before Todd came after them. Stopping in the middle of the hall, Howie looked around for a place to hide. He tried a few of the classroom doors, but they were all locked at this time of night. At last, he spotted their only option.

"Quick, hide in one of the empty lockers. These lockers are the unused ones, they won't be locked," Howie said in a whisper.

The two of them walked to separate lockers, quietly opening them and stepping inside. Slowly, they shut the locker doors and waited. What they needed right now was for Todd to go past them so they could escape. It was hard to fit in such a tight space, but Howie made it work, pushing himself against the back wall as far as he could. It was completely dark in the cramped space; the only source of light forced its way in through the slits of the door. Howie moved his face against one of the narrow openings and looked out into the deserted hallway. Cory was in one of the lockers on the other side of the hall, his eyes faintly visible from inside his locker. They waited. And for a moment, it looked like they may have avoided being noticed because nobody was following them. Howie considered risking it and opening his locker, but footsteps echoed from down the hall, getting louder with each step.

Slap...Slap...Slap...

From his viewpoint, Howie couldn't see who it was, but he assumed it was their crazed friend hunting them down. Todd had tried to tell him that Jessica Black made him do awful things, but part of him hadn't been able to believe it. It was all the proof he needed to know for sure Todd killed Mr. B. While it was Todd's body they had watched slaughter Mrs. Baxter, there was no way in hell it was their friend behind those eyes. She had taken full control of him.

Slap...Slap...Slap...

Howie held his breath as the steps drew nearer. He wanted to lean forward a little to get a better look in the direction of the noise, but he was too afraid to move and make a sound. The steps came to an abrupt stop. He heard the sound of a doorknob being turned, very close. He could hear a struggle as the door remained shut, and then a loud thump—the door being struck in frustration. Another moment of silence followed. Howie inhaled a deep breath and held still.

The sound of a locker getting slammed close by jolted Howie upright, causing his head to slam off the top of the locker. He just hoped it didn't blow his cover. One by one, the banging against the lockers continued to get louder, closer. A figure approached Howie's tiny viewport. Todd stopped, dead center in the hall, between his friends. He looked around, gripping his machete, and groaned.

"I know you guys are down here. Just come out and we can talk. What you saw back there wasn't me... she made me do it. She isn't in my head right now... I *promise*." Todd's tone was robotic behind the mask.

Todd turned toward the wall of lockers on Howie's side, and for the first time, Howie saw Todd's eyes behind the mask. It felt like they were staring through the locker directly at him.

The white of Todd's eyes had gone completely bloodshot. They were moving around abnormally, twitching side to side. Howie's body began to tremble, the thought of one of his best friends attempting to kill him was terrifying. Todd did not move, still looking right at the locker door Howie hid behind. It was a merciless game of chicken—who would react first?

"Whatever, I have bigger issues to worry about than you two," Todd said, walking past the lockers and continuing down the hall. Now that he was gone, Howie could see the locker Cory remained hidden in. He hoped Cory would wait before making a run for it.

Todd's footsteps started back up. Howie let out his breath and leaned back against the locker's wall. He didn't realize how tense his entire body had been until he went to move and his muscles cramped. He grabbed the handle, preparing to open it and run as fast as he could in the opposite direction of Todd. Something was wrong though—Todd's footsteps picked up speed and intensity. They were getting closer, not farther away.

Todd ran back into view, this time with his back to Howie, looking right at Cory's locker. He held up the machete and grabbed the locker door. Cory let out a scream and kicked the door into Todd, sending him flying back and charged out, slamming Todd into Howie's locker with a loud smack. Howie heard the clang of the machete dropping to the floor, then the struggle of his two friends wrestling around below his line of sight. He tried pushing the locker open, but it was stuck shut. The thumping sounds right outside explained why—Todd and Cory were pressed up against the door fighting one another on the floor.

"Hey, what's going on down there!" a voice from down the hall yelled.

"Mr. White! Help! Todd has lost his mind! He's trying to kill us!" Cory said while struggling to break free.

The echoes of more footsteps running down the hall; it sounded like Mr. White was running as fast as an old man with bad knees could run. Howie looked out through the slits and saw Cory getting up from the floor as Todd also came into view pushing Cory out of the way. Once again, Howie tried to push the locker open with no luck. It was jammed shut, the impact of Cory and Todd slamming into it must have bent the door inward.

"Help me out! The door's stuck shut!" Howie yelled.

Nobody seemed to be paying any attention to him, there were bigger concerns than a kid stuck in a locker. He looked on in helpless dismay. He watched as Todd ran for the machete, reaching down to grab it. Cory barreled into him, knocking him down. Mr. White appeared and attempted to restrain Todd on the floor.

"Quick, go and get Officer Miller, he's by the main lobby trying to help Mrs. Baxter," he said to Cory.

Cory looked at the locker Howie was stuck in, unsure of what to do. Howie kicked at the locker, trying to pry it open.

"What about Howie? He's stuck in there Mr. White, we need to help him out," he said pointing at the locker.

"He'll have to wait... we need to get Mr. Seymour detained before anyone else gets hurt. Now go!"

With one last look toward his best friend, Cory ran off down the hall to get Officer Miller. Howie felt helpless, like an animal stuck in a trap. Claustrophobia started to set in, the walls felt as if they were compressing. Sweat dripped down Howie's face into his eyes. He kicked at the door, but it was so tight in the condensed space that he could not get much force behind it.

"She's going to kill you all... For what you did to her. This is your fault!" Todd said hysterically.

What did he mean? What really happened to Jessica, and what would Mr. White have to do with it?

"Shut up, you little shit. You stab and kill a teacher and you have the nerve to say *I* did something wrong? What we did was to protect this town, Jessica was just the sacrifice to do that."

"You know that's bullshit, old man. I see things, she's in my head, I know exactly what happened. Your little Coven got bored and decided to explore other avenues beyond witchcraft. It was your idea to summon a demon. Jessica tried to stop you guys and got crossed up with the beast," Todd said while straining under the power of Mr. White.

"You're just some stupid little boy, you wouldn't know the first thing about sacrifice, or about greater powers. That was supposed to be the next step in advancing our Coven to become bigger, stronger than any before us had brought the group. *She* ruined that. Now we're in hiding like a bunch of Nazi war criminals because of her fuck up!"

It was hard to believe Mr. White would have said this had he remembered that Howie was in a locker right next to him. The back of his bald head was only a few feet in front of Howie, his skin turning a bright red while struggling to restrain Todd.

Multiple sets of footsteps came racing down the hall as Officer Miller and Cory arrived. Todd gave one last attempt at breaking free at the sight of the others coming, knocking Mr. White off, and getting up to run. Howie observed as Officer Miller took his baton and slammed it into the back of Todd's head, sending blood spatter against the locker and dropping Todd to the floor unconscious.

"What the hell Josh! Did you kill the kid?" Mr. White asked.

"Would you really care? He just slaughtered two adults—nobody would blink twice. I knew I should've locked the bastard up when I had him in the station. Donnie's lucky he was connected with us," Officer Miller said with a snarl. "Help me get him over to the stairs, I'm going to cuff him to the rail."

They grabbed Todd's limp body and dragged him out of Howie's view. Cory came running over to the locker, trying to force it open.

"Hold on man, I'm going to get you out of there."

Cory looked around for something to help pry it open and spotted the machete. He picked it up with a look of disgust when he saw all the blood.

"Watch out, I'm going to stick the blade in and try to pop the door open."

Howie moved his leg to the side, looking down to see the tip of the blade poke through the thin slice of light coming in. Cory grunted while putting his weight into the nudges. The door started to break free as a shout from the stairs rang out. Cory stopped prying and looked over in their direction.

"Oh shit, she's coming..."

Bang! Bang! Bang!

Three gunshots cracked through the hallway like a vicious thunderbolt. It was a deafening sound, setting off a powerful ringing noise in Howie's ears. Cory got back to work on the door, giving one last push and finally it popped open. The machete fell to the floor and Howie jumped out of the tight space. For a brief second, he felt relieved, taking a deep breath of fresh air. The relief drained when he looked over toward the stairs and saw Jessica crouched at the top of the second floor approaching. Officer Miller looked like he'd seen a ghost, backpedaling down the hall as he raised his gun toward her. He fired off three more erratic shots, one of them clipped Jessica in the shoulder and she hardly flinched.

"For fuck's sake! I need to reload, get somewhere safe!" he yelled to Mr. White.

Todd sat limp, his masked head hanging down, his arm handcuffed to the railing. Officer Miller fumbled around with his gun, trying to reload like someone handling a firearm for the first time. Jessica remained crouched at the top of the stairs, shifting her weight back slightly while her feet remained planted—like a catapult preparing to launch.

Mr. White slowly backed away, afraid to take his eyes off her. He felt around blindly for the closest classroom door with one hand, the other reaching for his keys. His clammy palm found the familiar shape of a doorknob, letting him know he had made it to a room. He glanced down at the keys and found the room number he was at. Looking back at Howie and Cory he said, "Get in here, it's your only chance…"

While they wanted to survive, the thought of going in there with Mr. White when it was clear that he was a target was not an attractive scenario.

He got the door open and backed into the classroom. He stood at the doorway for a second, waiting for them to follow him in. When they did not follow, he shook his head impatiently.

"Suit yourselves, it's your funeral," he said and slammed the door shut, locking it from the other side.

Officer Miller finished reloading his firearm and raised the gun again, preparing to fire. A guttural snarl escaped Jessica at the sight of the weapon. In an instant, she jumped from the second floor, launching herself at Miller below with such speed that he lost aim and his shots went wide. Before he could get off another shot, she was on him, viciously clawing at his face with her curled talons. He screamed in pain while she hooked her nails into the skin of his cheeks and ripped them apart. In a matter of seconds his face was unrecognizable. The screams were fading. Jessica snapped her head up toward Howie and Cory, sending a chill down Howie's spine. She let out a blood curdling scream at them, the strength of it pushing them back like an invisible forcefield. Jessica looked down at Officer Miller, his body convulsing and letting out soft moans as blood gurgled up out of his mouth. Ripping the claws from his face, she raised her hand high above her head and drove it down into his chest. A ripping noise, that sounded like fabric being torn apart, filled the hallway. Howie realized it wasn't the shirt making the sound, it was Miller's skin. The cop's feet kicked frantically, no longer trying to escape but twitching involuntarily with the intense pain.

"Run! We have to get her away from here—find a place to set the trap!" Howie said to Cory.

"The machete..." Cory looked toward the weapon, now too close to where Jessica held down Miller.

It was too much of a risk to try and grab the weapon, so they turned and ran. They reached the end of the wing and turned around to see if they were being followed. Jessica was crouched over Officer Miller, her face buried in his chest while her hands pried the skin away. They watched in shock as she tore the heart out of the lifeless body. The plan was falling apart by the second. Howie never expected Jessica to grow this strong so quickly. They grabbed their bags and took off down the hall.

He just hoped they still had a chance.

CHAPTER TWENTY-SEVEN

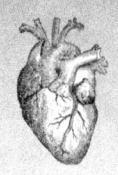

Brian White sat in the dark classroom, hiding in the far corner so that he couldn't be seen through the door's window. His doctor told him he should not push himself physically at his age. Exercise was a good thing, but his heart struggled in its weakened state, and putting too much strain on it could lead to a heart attack. At this moment, he would welcome that way of dying compared to the alternative. Sweat perspired from every inch of his body; his shirt stuck to his back, drenched. His joints throbbed—something that occurred just walking at a brisk pace these days, let alone running.

He looked around the room for anything to defend himself. The school had implemented very stern rules banning any objects that could be used as weapons from the classrooms, so unless he could beat Jessica to death with a ruler, he was screwed.

How did this happen? How did she escape?

The bastard kid in the hall had been right: she wanted him, and he knew it. Did they make mistakes? Sure. But they did what they felt necessary to protect the town, or more importantly, the Coven at the time. Keeping it all a secret had not been easy, but with the help of Officer Miller, they had managed to make it a thing of the past. It remained of utmost importance that their group stayed a secret. The truth, how the demon was summoned, how it got trapped in Jessica's body, all the death and mayhem that followed—it had been buried for twenty years, just like her body. He would stop at nothing to make sure a group of nosey kids did not uncover all the secrets they had worked so hard to cover up. He needed to notify the others that she was back, and that she would be coming for them. Officer Miller already knew that, of course; he found out the hard way. The moron thought a gun could end Jessica. A *gun*! Granted, there was a hierarchy within the Coven to obtain levels of magic, to study and learn the ways. Miller—while very important to protecting the hidden identity of the Coven—was too much of a hot head for the others to trust with such powers. Brian was the only remaining member to retain the necessary abilities to fend off Jessica. Once she finished with Miller's body, she would be on to her next victim, and Brian was not about to let that be him. He felt under his soaked shirt and located the talisman he had been wearing ever since the summoning. If she was going to come for him, he would make every effort to ward her off with the protection stone in the necklace, to buy himself enough time to escape.

The ticking of the clock broke the room's silence. He crouched in the corner like a scared little child, hoping, *praying* she would leave him alone. If he got out of here alive, he would be kissing this town goodbye. They could find someone else to run the damn school. The Coven remained on hiatus anyway; they agreed to lay low after the botched summoning. It had not been an easy decision, but they wanted to stay off the radar of the Feds after Henry had been taken away. Many of the original members had died of old age, some had been killed by Jessica before she was disposed of. Miller—now the latest to be added to the tally—made sure things stayed under wraps. Back when the original murders had taken place, her kills were cold and calculated, targeting members of the Coven only. What he witnessed outside was nothing of the sort. She now killed anything in her path, and there appeared to be no end in sight.

Brian took off his glasses and wiped the sweat from his eyes. Eventually he would have to make a run for it, balky knees or not. The thought of trying to escape through the window occurred to him, but at well over six feet tall, he knew there was no chance he would get all the way out. Getting stuck in a window with his ass hanging out while a demon-witch ripped his heart out would make great headlines in the local paper, hell probably even national news, but he would let someone else be the headline tonight. *Think damn it, think*!

In the back corner of each classroom, a door had been placed. These doors were there for safety in the event of something like a school shooter, to provide quick access from room to room without needing to go out in the hall. If he could just make it down to the last room, he could hopefully get out to the lobby and then out of the school for good. The kids could fend for themselves. The stupid shits wouldn't listen to him anyway.

Grabbing the set of keys, Principal White headed toward the back of the room, ready to make his escape. With his hands shaking, he fumbled around to get the right key to the next classroom. He did not dare glance over at the main door's window, in fear that Jessica would be staring back at him from the hall. The first key he tried did not work, so he pulled it out to try another. With the room swathed in darkness, it was tough to see the key numbers, especially with his bifocals on. He leaned down, squinting at the keys while he used the faint moonlight peeking in from the windows along the wall to try and get a better look at them. *Come on... where is the damn key?*

Finally, he found the key he needed and inserted it in the keyhole. He glanced over at the hallway door, unable to control his fearful curiosity—and saw nothing but a dark corridor through the small eye-level window. Maybe he was finally getting the break he needed to escape? Forcefully, he pushed the escape door open, quickly stopping it before it slammed into the wall of the next room. If he planned on getting out alive, he needed to work smarter, quieter. From here, there were only three more rooms to get through before he could make a run for it out into the main lobby area. With a brisk walk, Brian strode toward the door in the next room. Again, he grabbed the set of keys to open the second door. *Again,* he glanced over at the main door of the new room leading out into the hall. Only this time, it wasn't an emptiness he saw. Blood dripped down Jessica's chin onto her torn dress, her face inches from the glass, staring back at Brian.

"No... no, no, no!"

His hands were shaking so much, the keys might as well have been lathered in grease. Principal White attempted to put the next key in but dropped the set onto the floor. A loud, violent thud came from Jessica's direction, forcing him to look over. She was attempting to break through the door, and he could see her swiping her powerful claws against the wooden frame. The door began to break, each strike sending splinters flying.

"Stay away from me! You left us no choice, Jessica!"

A sharp pain shot through his knees bending down to pick up the keys. The pain took a backseat in his mind. He swiped them up and started trying random keys one after the other, too distraught to take the time to find the right one. Jessica was close to breaking through the door, he was running out of time. Brian desperately stuck the next key in and turned. The most beautiful sound he had ever heard followed, the click of the lock setting free. This time, he didn't concern himself with making noise, the door slammed into the wall as he plowed through to the next classroom at the same moment Jessica broke through the main door. Had he been thinking logically, he would have shut the door behind him and locked it to buy himself more time. Unfortunately, the thought to do that only came after he realized he had left it wide open behind him and saw her entering the classroom hot on his trail. He turned around, watching her step into the room, her bare feet slapping off the tile floor as she walked toward him in a confident stride.

"What do you want from me? You did this to yourself! You should've never tried to stop the summoning you... you bitch!"

He knew he was not talking to Jessica anymore. She died when Henry buried her. What he stared at was a demon trapped in her dead body. A demon who was pissed off for being confined in the ground for two decades. Brian slowly backed up toward the next door, half-heartedly trying to prepare the next key. He could always try to make a run for it to the main entrance of the classroom and escape out into the hallway, but he knew she would be too quick for him and cut him off before he got there. Again, he looked around for anything that could defend him, anything to give him more time. He grabbed a stapler off the teacher's desk and heaved it at her as she stood in the opening. It felt as if she was toying with him, feeding off the panic. The stapler flew by her head, yet she remained unfazed and continued to march toward him.

As she got closer, he could see her skin in detail. It had started to peel from her body, rotting away. The stench coming from it was nauseating, burning his nostrils with a smell of decaying meat. He grabbed a paperweight off the desk and again threw it at her. This time he connected, the weight smacked into her chest, tearing a hole in the dead skin. On a normal body, blood would have run from the wound, but nothing escaped the gash. *What am I doing here? This won't stop her.*

In a last-ditch effort to save himself, the principal grabbed ahold of the two closest desks and threw them down in front of her, hoping to slow her down. He turned and stuck a key in the next door. He was so close to getting out and never seeing this town again.

The key clicked into place, and he let out a sigh of relief. He could sense her closing in but did not dare turn around to see how close she stalked behind. Her warm, rancid breath spread across the back of his neck. It didn't make any sense, for at most she had to be just over five feet, and he towered over most people who stood next to him. How could she be breathing on his neck? Sharp claws pierced the back of his head, and he let out a scream. Her grip tightened, squeezing down with an immortal strength. It felt like his head was going to pop open, the pressure unbearable.

Hello, Brian... It's time you pay for your mistakes. I am going to enjoy feasting on your heart, very much so...

"No! Please, I'll do whatever you need me to! It was their idea anyway, not mine!"

No time for excuses, old man...

Brian wanted to say something, but he could not get the words out. He quickly grabbed for the talisman and yanked it off his neck. The claws in the back of his head detracted as she backed off with a hiss. Brian quickly turned around, holding the stone up toward her, watching as her snarl intensified at the sight of it.

"You think I wasn't prepared for this, demon?"

Jessica looked to his trembling hand holding the protection stone, then back to his eyes. With one quick swipe, she swatted it out of his hand, sending it flying across the classroom. Brian turned back, attempting to get the next door open in one last desperate attempt to save himself. Before he could make another move, the sensation of her claws puncturing into the back of his head returned. His head jerked back with such force, he thought he heard a crack in his neck as he looked straight up at the ceiling. Jessica slowly leaned over and looked down at him with a sadistic smile on her face. Her hand was firmly locked to the back of his skull. A warm sensation moved down Brian's leg; he realized he had just pissed himself in fear. She squeezed the back of his head tighter, ripping the skin from his skull, then slammed his face into the door's window with a shattering crack. Shards of glass exploded out from his glasses; the frames cutting into his eyes. The window splintered, and again she rammed his face into it, smashing his head through the opening. As she pulled his head back out, pieces of jagged glass stuck out of his face, blood trickling down into his eyes. He moaned, unable to get any words out. And with that, Jessica dropped his body limply to the floor. *Is she letting me go?*

It was wishful thinking, and he knew it. The back of his head felt like someone had ferociously pounded it with the claws of a hammer, pain throbbing with each beat of his heart. *My heart.* The thought of it left a knot in the pit of his stomach. She intended to eat his damn heart, and he was coming to the realization that his life might be about to end. Moving was not possible, his body stuck in a state of paralysis, the glass had blinded him, so all he could do was wait in darkness for her to end it.

I am going to make you suffer, you wrinkled old scum. You can live long enough to feel your own beating heart torn out of your chest...

That was the last thing Brian White heard.

CHAPTER TWENTY-EIGHT

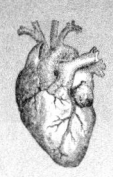

Howie burst through the gym doors, panting uncontrollably. Cory followed him in and everyone looked at them, waiting for them to speak. They planned to tell the students to take off. Now that Jessica hunted at the other end of the school, they would have time to escape. The words would not come out, however. He realized that half the kids in here suffered from some sort of injury and would not be able to escape on foot. But they had no choice if they wanted any chance to live, these students needed to get out of here now.

"Everyone... she's at the other end of the school. Get out of here now, take a car, bike, whatever you can and go!" Howie yelled.

At first, nobody moved. They all sat around in shock; his statement looked to have no effect on them. Bethany ran over to them, hugging Cory before speaking.

"I"ll get them out of here... did Officer Miller find you? He's the only one with a gun," she said.

Cory looked at her, tears sliding down his cheeks. "She...

she killed him. And I think she killed Mr. White too... and Razor Ray," he trailed off, crying.

"Oh no," Bethany said covering her mouth. "Okay, we got this, we're getting out of here alive. Let's get to work on rounding these kids out of here."

Cory shook his head. "No, we need to finish this Bethany, only we know how to stop her."

She looked at him without saying a word, her eyes watering up.

"There's no time to debate, you have to get them out of here," Cory said.

Bethany nodded, taking one last glance at them, and ran off toward the crowd. She yelled, pushed, and did whatever it took, but it finally started sinking in with everyone. They all started to get up and run toward the exit and out into the parking lot. One by one, students exited the gym and got one step closer to safety.

All this bouncing back and forth made Howie realize how imperfect their plan truly was. First, they told everyone to get to the gym, now they wanted them to leave the gym. They chased after Jessica, now they found themselves running away from her. Howie wished Mr. B was still around to help. He would have had a plan with more structure than a couple kids trying to come up with one on the fly. It felt as if the world's biggest weight sat on his shoulders, and it all started because he had been too afraid to tell his parents in fear that his dad would hurt him again. It was selfish, and now he realized he put himself above everyone else, above his friends. That included his best friend, who had held onto more secrets than anyone through their entire friendship. Cory knew about Howie's dad, about his history of violence at the first hint of something going wrong. The bond that formed between the two of them remained unbreakable after all they had been through. He looked over at Cory, hoping that when this was all done, his friend would forgive him for all of this.

"Okay, let's get outside and hopefully this freak will follow us. There's no turning back now," Cory said, looking unconvinced.

"Cory... I'm really sorry about everything man. I put you guys through so much just to hide this from my dad, this could've all been prevented if we acted sooner."

Cory looked away, unable to make eye contact with Howie. "Howie, any of us woulda done the same thing in your shoes. I can't even imagine what it's like living every day in fear."

They headed out the door and saw everyone getting in cars and driving away. A small silver lining in the worst night of their life: the rest of the students would get away unharmed. Howie wished he could say the same about himself and Cory.

✟

Ryan exited the machine shop with an upgrade. His wooden bat wouldn't do much damage, but he held out hope that the sharp metal pole he found in the scrap pile would provide better protection. The pole was four feet long with a sharp tip on one end he hoped to stab in the witch's eye. While he felt bad for Jessica and what the Coven members had done to her, he also knew that this was no longer some innocent young woman who happened to join a cult and realize she made a mistake. Jessica was long dead. What remained was the demon that the Coven summoned and trapped in her body. His dad had been forced to help cover up the whole thing by Officer Miller and his bully crew. It all made sense now, why they had been forced to stay away from the woods, why after all this time the body remained missing until they broke the rules and went in the woods to film their movie.

His dad had been a hero, and while it initially stung to hear his mom say that he took part in the coverup, when she explained why, it took some of the sting away. It still upset Ryan to think his parents hid this from him all these years. They built a relationship on trust, a bond tighter than any friendship he could ever have. While he was hurt by his dad's secret, he understood why he kept it buried all these years. The pressure he must have felt to keep something like that from his son, who he told everything to, must have crushed him. Ryan needed to avenge his dad's death, take her down once and for all.

Something was different when he walked in the direction of the lobby. The sounds of all the kids going crazy had disappeared; the school now dead silent. He didn't like it. Was he too late? Had she killed everyone in sight? Ryan picked up the pace and rounded the corner into the lobby. The bodies of Razor Ray and Mrs. Baxter lay sprawled out in a pool of their own blood. If not for seeing ample amounts of dead bodies tonight, he probably would have screamed in shock. Unfortunately, he had seen things no kid should ever set eyes on.

He looked down the wing closest to him, mostly dark besides the lone flickering light at the end of the stairwell. Officer Miller's body lay on the floor, mutilated far worse than the two he stood next to. The puddles of blood looked fresh. Besides the cop's body, the hall was empty.

Ryan shook his head and jogged to the front entrance, heading out into the parking lot. Most of the cars were gone, a few students still scurrying to find a way out. He felt some relief to see so many getting away—there had been far too many casualties of the bloodbath tonight. Staying close to the building, Ryan jogged in a crouched position, prepared to act at the first sight of Jessica. As he got around to the bonfire, he still saw no sign of her. *Where the hell did she go?* He stood there, looking at the flames and how they went about their business undisturbed. That was when he heard footsteps coming up behind him. He spun around quickly, expecting to see a demon. Instead, he saw a prick. Matt, mister big shot athlete and school bully, stood directly behind him.

"Hey, fat ass. What are you doing out here all alone? Did you have something to do with all of this?"

After everything he had been through the last few days, he no longer felt fazed by someone talking down to him like this. There were far bigger worries than some jock who would likely never leave his hometown, thinking he held a spot above everyone.

"Matt, what the fuck. Save your crap for another day, okay?"

"See, I want to, fatty. I want to let it go, let you run and cry to your mommy. The problem is that my car was stolen by one of the other pussies who fled. So, give me your keys and I won't beat the shit out of you tonight... I'll *save it for another day* as you say."

"No," Ryan said, gritting his teeth. He tightened his grip on the metal bar.

"Excuse me? It wasn't an option, Tits. Give me the damn keys now."

"You think you can just bully your way through life, huh? That everyone will bow to the great Matt. Look around, man. Half the school's dead, you can drop the big tough guy gimmick."

"I tried to let you go, guess I was being too nice."

Matt charged toward Ryan and stopped in his tracks

when he saw Ryan raise the metal bar like a bat, ready to swing.

"You think that scares me? You couldn't hit a ball off a tee," he snickered.

He sounded more confident than he looked. The fire crackled and popped next to them, burning Ryan's cheek and hand closest to the blaze with an uncomfortable warmth. Ryan was tempted to move away from the fire to lessen the discomfort of the heat, but he was afraid any sudden move and Matt would charge again. He saw movement behind Matt and his eyes opened wide.

"Matt... she's behind you. Just run, now!"

Matt laughed and shook his head. "Nice try, you aren't getting off that easy."

When he saw Ryan frozen in place terrified, he glanced back over his shoulder. Jessica hovered a few feet off the ground, the fire giving her body an orange glow. It wasn't just the fact that she was floating in the air that scared the hell out of Ryan; her skin was starting to peel away from her body like a rotten banana peel. The flames were not touching her, yet their heat began melting the skin away. Matt backed toward Ryan, keeping an eye on Jessica while she slowly rose higher above.

"What... the... fuck!" Matt yelled, bumping into Ryan. "Watch it, Ryan. Get the hell out of my way!"

And with that, Jessica shot forward with such force they had no time to react. She slammed into both of them, sending them sprawling to the ground. Ryan rolled over and saw Matt crawling, trying to get to his feet and take off. Jessica stood over him. The metal bar had flown from Ryan's hands when he hit the ground, out of reach. Ryan got up, ran over and grabbed it. When he looked back, Jessica had lifted Matt off the ground with one hand. Her claws dug into his back as he screamed. If Ryan could separate the two of them somehow, there might be a shot that he could push her into the fire and burn her to a pile of dust.

"Hey witch! Come and get me!" Ryan yelled.

Jessica snapped her head toward him, still holding Matt's flailing body. His movements slowed and came to a stop. He had passed out from the pain and was oblivious to what was going on. Ryan decided he couldn't waste another moment, charging at her with the sharp end of the blade aimed right at Jessica's head.

It was as if she was five steps ahead of him, ready for every move.

She swatted the bar from Ryan's grip with her free hand, and screamed in his face, forcing him to fall backwards. Grabbing the back of Matt's head, she violently slammed his face into a burning log poking out of the fire, lodging it into his skull. His hair immediately lit up in a blaze. The sounds coming from his quivering body made Ryan sick to his stomach. The smell of burning meat hit his nostrils as the fire began to take to the flesh. He looked back at Jessica who was now staring right at him. He had got his wish; she had her full attention on him now. The skin on her arms was now hanging off. Underneath, Ryan could see muscle and bone. The lack of blood gave the muscle a strange grayish-purple color. Again, he grabbed the bar and charged at her, knowing she would be ready for him. He lowered his shoulder, trying to take her down low like they had taught him the summer he decided to try playing football. He had been talked into it because of his size, but the entire locker room—including Matt who was now just a piece of overdone meat—picked on him every chance they got. It had been the worst two weeks of his life before he quit the team, and that was saying a lot. But the technique finally came in handy: he stabbed the sharp end of the bar into her leg, and she shrieked in anger.

His eyes were turned down as he pushed with all his strength to get her closer to the fire. They were now so close that he could feel warmth on his face, like a bad sunburn blistering his pale skin. Sweat dripped into his eyes, but he fought through the stinging pain and pushed on. Jessica raked both of her hands down his back, knocking the wind out of him and dropping him. Ryan understood this was likely where his life would end, but he was at peace with that. If he could end her, avenge his dad, save his friends, that would all be worth it. The fire was less than a foot behind her, he was so close to forcing her in. *So close.* Something didn't feel right, his feet were no longer pushing on the ground, it felt like they were floating. He realized Jessica was lifting him off the ground, all two hundred plus pounds of him, like he was a stuffed animal. He grabbed onto the pole sticking out of her leg, holding on for dear life as she tried to lift him higher. His fingers were slipping, his grip on the bar was loosening. When his hands came completely free, Jessica pulled him up to be eye level with her. It was obvious that she was finally at full strength, holding him up by the back of his shirt. The fabric started to rip, and he felt himself starting to break free, but then her claws stabbed into his back and pinned him in place. Ryan winced and lifted his eyes to look directly at her.

"Burn... in Hell, bitch!"

He pulled back his head and drove a headbutt right into the center of Jessica's nose. Her head jerked back, and her claws retracted from his skin, dropping him to the ground. The slight kickback of her head got her hair within reach of the fire, instantly setting it alight like the end of a torch. She shrieked as the fire spread across the back of her skull. Her head swung side to side, instinct kicking in to try and put the fire out before it was too late.

Ryan took advantage of her lapse in focus and charged at her, plowing his shoulder into her midsection, and sending them both into the blaze. Jessica fell completely in, collapsing through a half-burned pile of wooden pallets that had been laid down earlier in the night. Ryan landed on top of her and the pain of his skin charring beneath the fire was excruciating. His eyes felt like they might melt out of his skull.

He jumped back out of the fire and rolled around on the ground, trying anything to get the fire out and stop the burning. The flames slowly dissipated, but he could feel his nerves still pulsing, sending every kind of signal to his brain to just *make the pain stop*. He turned his head toward the fire and watched the remaining pallets settle in place on top of her body. *I did it, I got her Dad,* he thought, and then everything went black.

CHAPTER TWENTY-NINE

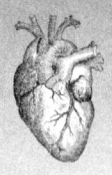

The last of the cars pulled out of the school parking lot as Howie and Cory watched them flee to safety. Only Bethany remained with them, which made Howie respect her even more than he already did. Here was one of the most popular girls in school, someone that could easily scoff at talking with the likes of Howie and Cory, and instead she agreed to be in their crap horror movie, be friends with them, and help make sure everyone got to safety before she did. In a town where popularity and politics mattered, she couldn't have cared less. She looked at them as the last set of taillights shrank into the distance, and forced a smile.

"Well, that's everyone. Are you sure I can't convince you guys to come with me and get out of here while you still can?"

Cory shook his head, unsure of what to say next. "We have to do this Bethany. We're the reason she's here, and we are the only ones who know how to end it…"

"That's such bullshit, Cory! It's not your fault she was out there in the first place. How would you have known?"

"I know, but it happened. And here we are. Listen, I plan on getting out of here alive. But I want to make sure I get the chance to say it..." Cory trailed off. "Fuck it, what's there to be shy about anymore? I've had a crush on you since sixth grade. Yeah, I know most guys have had a crush on you so it's not something new to you, but I just wanted you to know that. I think you are perfect—"

She interrupted him with a kiss. They held each other for a moment—too long considering how short on time they were, Howie thought, but he kept his mouth shut and let his best friend have his moment. When she pulled away, she was crying. She shook her head at him.

"I hate that you are being so stubborn about this, but I get it. Let me come with you guys and help," she said.

"Nope. Absolutely not. You need to get out of here. We have the plan all figured out," Cory lied.

She started to argue, but she saw in Cory's eyes he would not change his mind. As much as she wanted to go with them, she didn't want to distract them either. She kissed him on the forehead and opened her car door.

"I hope you know what you're doing guys. Howie, bring him back in one piece, will you?"

Howie said nothing, watching as she shut her car door and drove out of the parking lot. They had already wasted too much time, and they needed to find Jessica Black and put an end to the madness. Before either of them could say anything, a deafening squeal, like someone stabbing a giant pig, came from where the bonfire burned. They turned and ran, recognizing Jessica, and she sounded pissed.

The fire burned up ahead, now blazing at least fifteen feet high. Weaving in and out of the bodies and fender benders, Howie and Cory got to the edge of the fire and looked around. When they saw nothing, they walked around the perimeter of the bonfire, looking for any sign of her. What they did not expect to find was a body hanging from a log, roasting in the flames. There was no way to see who it was, the body had been burned to a crisp. Howie glanced around and spotted Ryan on the ground, covered head to toe in burns.

"Oh my god, Ryan!" he yelled and ran to his friend.

As he got closer, he saw that Ryan was still breathing, but for how long was anyone's guess. His clothes had been seared into his skin; the camouflage of his pants was mostly black—at least where any fabric remained. Holes had burned through the pants, appearing like giant cigarette burns that revealed skin which had begun to pus through the bubbles brought on by the extreme heat. The left side of his face looked like something Freddy Kruger would cringe at. Howie kneeled next to Ryan, not sure if he should try to move him or not.

"Hey man, can... can you hear me?" He nudged Ryan on the side that had escaped severe burns.

A crazed moan escaped Ryan's throat as he tried to force himself awake. His right eye opened, blinking uncontrollably—and then he screamed, whether it was fear, pain, or a mix of both, Howie was not sure. Ryan attempted to move and let out another scream, this one was clearly one of agony.

"Don't move man, stay there. We'll get you help. We have to take care of this first, but I promise we will be back," Howie said.

Ryan wanted to respond, but half of his mouth had been melted shut. He looked toward the fire and pointed with his right arm.

"I... got her. It's... over," he mumbled through gritted teeth.

Howie looked toward the flames, which had engulfed everything around, making it hard to see anything. He held up his hand to block the heat that forced itself against their unprotected skin. Still, he didn't see anything in the fire. He looked back at Ryan, whose eye began rolling in the back of his head. His breathing turned to forced, strenuous gasps.

"Ryan, I'm so, so sorry about everything. I know all you ever wanted was to be friends, to have fun and forget about all the shit you got put through every day. I'm sorry that we were not better to you. When your dad died, we didn't even hang around for you when you lost the person you cared most about..." Howie started crying, wiping away the tears as he watched Ryan fading.

Cory walked up and put his hand on Howie's shoulder and started crying himself.

"Bud, we messed up. You deserved better than what we put into this friendship. You were always there for us when shit hit the fan, but we rarely returned the favor. Like Howie said, we're sorry..."

Ryan's breathing slowed, he opened his eye again and looked up at the sky. His eye filled with tears, his lips trembling.

"Da... dad... *Dad*?"

Howie looked up at the sky with the moon shining down on them and saw a sky littered with stars. He turned back to Ryan and noticed his chest no longer moving to the strained rhythm from seconds before.

"Ryan? Buddy?" he asked numbly.

A blank stare looked through him, and Howie lost it. He cried deep from within, deeper than he thought possible. Ryan was gone. And he'd sacrificed himself to save them, to end Jessica's reign of terror. Howie felt empty inside, dazedly getting to his feet and backing away from the fire. Cory followed him, taking one last look at their friend before walking away.

"So, it's over... she's gone?" Cory asked.

Howie didn't answer, too caught up in the moment to say anything. They stood by the stage and sat on its edge in silence. The crackle of the fire echoed through the parking lot, almost becoming an everyday sound. He wasn't sure how long they sat there, but it felt like they had been there forever when Howie finally looked up from his daze. The way the flames danced around, shooting up in different directions, began changing. He focused on the center of the fire, trying to figure out what looked different. Cory saw him inspecting it and joined in to see what was drawing Howie's attention. From the embers of the fire's core, the outline of a figure rose, impossible to make out through the orange and blue sparks. Slowly, the body walked out of the fire, still engulfed in flames. Blackened like tar, she would have been unidentifiable if not for the long claws that hung from each hand. That, and the orange eyes. Those awful, terrifying eyes that'd haunted them for the last week. Her hair had been burned away, revealing a scalp that looked like it had been shoved through a meat grinder. She peered around at the chaos she had created, and then locked her eyes on them. In that moment, Howie just wanted to be home, in his bed, hiding. Whatever his dad might do to him would not compare to this.

"We have to move, Howie! Let's go!" Cory said as he jumped off the platform and headed toward the woods.

Snapping out of it, Howie jumped up and followed Cory away from the stage. They stopped, looking around for a place to go. Howie scanned the area, and then looked up at the ski jump poking out over the treetops. An idea struck him, one he hoped would save their lives if they got moving. He took off toward the hill leading into the forest. Jessica—or whatever that thing was—confidently stalked toward them. The hill may have provided a steep incline, but they ran up it like it was nothing, adrenaline pushing them on. When they arrived at the top of the hill, Howie looked back down and saw Jessica approaching the bottom. The flames cleaving to her had mostly extinguished, leaving her black silhouette hidden by nightfall. Her burning eyes and sharp white teeth were a different story, standing out even from atop the hill. They turned and ran, the massive structure of the ski slope sitting just up ahead of them, stretching toward the stars. In this area, the trees had been cut down to make room for the slope. For the moment, the light of the moon guided them. As if the night could get any eerier, the full moon dominating the sky cast the forest in a ghostly shade of blue. Howie and Cory arrived at the base of the jump and stopped.

"We have to climb it, Cory. Think about it, it's the only spot out here where we can get her secluded, otherwise we're out in the open for her," Howie said between breaths.

"This is a fucking death trap, Howie."

"Well, unless you have any better ideas it's the only spot to get her cornered."

Cory shook his head and walked to the ladder on the side of the jump. The structure had not been used for a number of years, and it was obvious. Rust had eroded the metal support beams as well as the ladder. Cory put his hand on the first rung and looked back at Howie.

"Wonderful, this thing feels like it will fall apart just climbing slow, what if we need to move quickly?" Nonetheless, Cory started climbing.

When he got far enough up, Howie followed. It was a slow, steady climb—one where neither of them wanted to look down. Howie glanced below anyway and immediately regretted it. He'd never thought he feared heights, but he was second guessing that right now. Down below, he could see jagged ends of trees sticking out of the ground after their top half had fallen beneath years of New England weather taking its toll. A sick thought crossed his mind that the broken pieces looked like the ground's teeth, awaiting victims to fall so it could chew them up.

Cory finally reached the top and climbed up on the platform. At most, the floor up here extended five to six feet in each direction. Its only purpose had been for skiers to stand on it while they awaited their descent down the ramp before jumping off into the field below. A four-foot wall surrounded the floor on each side. *Thank God for small favors*, Cory thought. The wall added a small level of security to them from falling off the sides, but there was no wall heading down the ramp in front of him leading to the end of the jump. A fall down the steep decline would more than likely kill someone, or at the very least it would severely injure them. He turned on his flashlight and aimed the beam of light down at the floor. The wood had not aged well, even rotting in some places. Some of the floorboards felt squishy below his feet from years of rainfall.

Howie reached the top and looked around at the unstable structure. A blast of doubt struck him all at once. Would this even work? Why would they try to get her up here and not somewhere else? Whatever doubt he carried, he needed to let it go. If they didn't take her down, then Ryan would have died for nothing. Mr. B would have died for nothing.

Jessica didn't waste her time climbing the hill. From this viewpoint, they could see her hovering, gliding toward them from down below. As they watched her approach, a clanging noise from the ladder caught their attention.

Someone was climbing, and it wasn't Jessica. Confused, Cory ran over to see what was going on.

Howie knew he needed to be quick. He took off his

backpack and opened it, taking out the supplies he'd grabbed from Mr. B's house. In a moment of panic, he struggled to remember what the Devil's trap looked like. The doubt made it difficult to concentrate, but with Jessica getting close, and something else approaching, he forced himself to do his best. The salt container remained about half full, he prayed it was enough to do the full star. Quickly, he made a circle with the salt, wide enough to leave almost no room for Jessica to avoid it. Then, he attempted to make the best star he could in its center, recalling the pentagram from the video. When he was almost done, he looked back to Cory.

"What's going on over there?"

"I don't know, I can't see anything down there, it sounds like—"

Cory leaned his head over the side of the wall, and something struck him in the face. His body fell back into the Devil's trap. Todd popped up into view and climbed onto the platform. He no longer wore the mask, making his crazed eyes easier to see. The machete shone lethally, once again resided in his hand. Cory regretted dropping it after letting Howie out of the locker. He walked toward Cory ready to strike with the weapon.

Howie saw Todd raising the weapon and charged toward him. The last thing he wanted to do was take his eyes off Jessica, but his best friend was about to be slaughtered. Todd turned his attention to Howie and tried to sidestep quickly and avoid the contact. A sudden crack escaped from the floorboard, sending Todd's foot down through a newly formed hole in the rotted wood. He yelled as his knee buckled and dropped the machete. Taking advantage of the mishap, Howie swung a fist, popping Todd in the eye. Of all the reasons he'd envisioned punching Todd in the face, he'd never expected to do it because Todd was trying to kill them.

Todd dropped to the floor, holding his face, his leg still caught in the hole. It was as if the impact had brought him back to reality. He looked at Howie, unsure of what just happened.

"Guys... I can't control it. She's forcing me to do stuff, you need to get away from me before it's too late! Please... I've already done enough..."

Howie ran over and picked up the machete, instantly feeling safer with it in his hand. The moonlight gleamed off the blood that now caked the blade—the blood of so many people that only a few days ago Howie had seen walking the halls of the school. He looked back at Todd who was trying to get his leg free. It could have been far worse, but his leg had fallen through all the way up to his thigh. Instinct told Howie to go help him and get them all out of there. It was just too much of a risk, Todd could snap again at any moment.

"Keep an eye on him, Cory. I need to see where she went," Howie said.

Being careful to avoid any more dead boards, Howie moved back to the edge of the platform and looked down to find Jessica. She was nowhere to be seen. *Shit, where did she go?* Her tar-black appearance didn't help the situation; the moon could only shine so bright.

He scanned the area, looking for any sign that she might still be approaching. A scraping sound emitted from somewhere below, but he couldn't see anything down at the base of the jump. The noise started getting louder, like it was slowly getting closer to the top. And then, as if he needed a reminder, the orange eyes appeared on the side of the wooden frame about halfway down. She was climbing the side of the ski jump like some sadistic Spider-man.

"She's coming! Get ready...Cory?"

He got no response, so Howie turned around to look. Todd was out of the hole and strangling Cory with a ferocious grip, grinding the broken end of the handcuff that remained on his wrist into Cory's forehead. Gasping for air, Cory swung towards Todd's face, trying to break free. Howie had a decision to make—help Cory or prepare for Jessica as she inched closer to the top of the jump. It was the hardest decision he had ever had to make.

Jessica didn't give him time to make that decision himself. The scraping sound was so close, it sounded like she was already at the top. He looked down at her, the black figure twitching up the side with unnatural speed. She let out a low growl and launched herself, flying airborne over the wall and landing on the platform. Howie felt the foundation shake with the impact. The struggle continued behind him, but Howie was solely focused on the demon now standing in front of him. She walked closer, only a few feet out of reach.

Cory gouged Todd's eyes with his thumbs, desperate to relieve the pressure around his throat. Todd cried out, letting go of Cory and attempted to swat his hands away. The platform was so condensed, the four of them had almost no space to move around. Cory pushed Todd away and jumped to his feet, taking deep breaths to regain some of the oxygen he had been deprived.

"Todd... stop it man, don't listen to her! We can stop her if you just give us a chance!" Cory said.

Todd rubbed his eyes and snarled at Cory. "Fuck you! You would do the same thing if she was in your head! It is the only way to relieve the pain."

He ran at Cory, pushing him up against the side of the platform. Cory could feel himself being driven up against the wall, close to falling over the side. With a quick spin, he reversed their positions and had Todd against the unstable boards.

"I don't want to do this! Just stop, Todd! Please."

A shimmer of understanding appeared in Todd's face, like he finally registered what his friend was saying to him. Cory thought he had finally got through to him, and then Todd shoved Cory to the floor and kicked him in the face. As he lay on the ground, Cory looked up and thought he was about to die. But it didn't happen. Instead, Todd ran past him, plowing into the side of Jessica as she walked toward Howie. Jessica was far more powerful than him, but she did not see it coming and slammed into the wall, cracking the wooden frame.

"Get out of here you guys, I got this!" Todd yelled.

Howie was in disbelief, watching as Todd attempted to push her over the side of the steep structure. She roared out in frustration and slammed her claws into Todd's back, lifting him in one, foul swoop above her head. There was a brief second where Todd looked into Howie's eyes, sorrow and guilt looking back, and then he was thrown over the side of the wall, dropping below.

"No!" Howie yelled and charged to the side, momentarily forgetting about Jessica. He looked down just as Todd's body was impaled on a jagged tree. The sound of it forcing itself through his body was sickening, a loud splat that could be heard even from this high up. For the second time in a matter of minutes, Howie stared at the dead body of one of his best friends. After all Jessica had put Todd through, he still tried to fight through it to save them. But now he was dead.

"Howie, look out!" Cory said, snapping Howie's attention back to the platform.

He turned just as Jessica swiped at him, catching the

bottom of his jaw with one of her nails. The impact sent him flying against the wall, breaking free one of the boards which fell to the ground below. The force sent the machete flying, the weapon skidding down the slope well out of reach. She marched toward him, but there was nowhere for him to go. She was inches from the Devil's star, if they could just get her into it, maybe they could defeat her... Unfortunately, Howie was backed into the unstable wall, cornered by a monster that had one thing on its mind. Jessica now stood over him. The smell coming off her crisp, blackened body was wretched, reminding Howie of the time his mom left the turkey in the oven too long on Thanksgiving. It had stunk up the entire house for days—his dad never let her hear the end of it. The charred body cracked with her movements, displaying raw, pink flesh beneath the burnt outer layer.

She struck Howie with a sharp, piercing blow to the shoulder, sending an intense pain down his entire arm. Tears welled up in his eyes as he saw his life flashing before him. After all this, they were failing. Jessica lifted him up high with one easy motion, his feet dangling over the void. He was unsure if she was planning to throw him over the side, or tear him apart, but either way it was clear she was about to end his life. Howie was not a religious kid, but he closed his eyes and prayed with every ounce of energy he could, begging whoever was listening to help him. When he opened his eyes, Jessica had her other hand pulled back, preparing to strike.

Cory yelled out an angry roar as he ran up behind her, stabbing her with the machete in the back. She dropped Howie, almost sending him over the edge. Turning around, more agitated than hurt, Jessica shrieked at Cory and swiped with such a sudden force. He had no time to dodge. Blood shot from his chest as he fell backwards into the

Devil's Trap. She paid no attention to the circle, approaching Cory to finish the job.

"Now!" Cory screamed, as her feet stepped into the circle.

Howie jumped up and pulled the machete free from her back, the blade sliding out much smoother than he expected. Jessica arched her back and spun around. An anger Howie had never seen before looked back at him. She opened her mouth wide—a cracking sound escaping as the burned skin split apart—and went to move toward him.

She looked confused, unable to come any closer. When she looked down and saw that they had trapped her, she screamed in rage, trying to swipe at him. Howie remained out of her range, trying to get a good shot with the machete. Cory got up, still in the circle with her, and jumped on her back. He grabbed onto her arm, trying to hold it back so Howie could get closer. Jessica yanked the arm down, pulling Cory up and over her shoulder. He slammed down onto the platform with a loud thud, knocking the wind out of him. She stuck her foot on his chest and pushed down, her sharp toenails digging into his torso.

Howie lifted the machete, ready to strike. "Hey, Jessica!"

As she turned back to him, Howie swung the blade, aiming right at her neck. For a brief second, it stuck in the middle of her throat, and then forced its way out the other side. Her head flew off, spinning through the air and going over the side of the ski jump. The headless body stood in place for a few seconds before dropping to its knees and falling back onto Cory. Howie wandered to the wall and looked down, faintly making out the head down at the base. From here it looked like a giant piece of coal.

"Get this thing off of me!" Cory said.

Howie turned back, seeing Cory trying to crawl out

THE CURSED AMONG US

from under her body. While he was alive, Cory was in a great deal of pain. His chest had been torn open; the blood continued to flow out. He would need medical attention, but thankfully he appeared to have escaped major injury.

Howie felt lightheaded and sat down. Everything they had been through hit him at once. Off in the distance, the flickering of blue and red lights danced on the side of the brick building down below. The sounds of sirens soon followed. Howie could only assume someone fleeing the school went and got help. The two of them sat at the top of the ski jump, watching police arrive in the parking lot. He wasn't really sure what they would tell the authorities, or what they would even believe. Eventually they would have to go down and face the questions, and then face their parents. Cory would be okay, his mom would make sure he was taken care of, make sure he was nurtured the way a kid should be after a traumatic event. Howie however, he knew he was going home to face a demon of a different nature. He thought how in the movies, you always see the hero walk away happy, being applauded for saving everyone. Nothing was going to change in his household. Sure, his mom would break down in tears and hug him, his dad might even hug him once after hearing what happened. But when all was said and done, his dad was still his dad. It wasn't something he could help. An anger fueled his dad—deep down inside—that he could not control. Howie felt the urges inside himself sometimes and hoped that when he was a parent someday that he wouldn't treat his kids the same way his dad treated him. The hard truth was that there were real life monsters that would never go away.

Down below, Howie watched a few officers walking up to the fire, approaching Ryan's body. *Poor Ryan*. He had done everything to try and be the best friend he could to them. They all ribbed each other every day, just like any group of boys tends to do. But he never really stopped to think about how much harder Ryan took it than they did. He wished he could go back in time and fix it. Treat Ryan the way he deserved to be treated, like the friend he really was. All he could do now was hope that somewhere Ryan knew this. That he knew how grateful they were. One thing was for sure. Their lives, and the town of Newport, would never be the same.

EPILOGUE

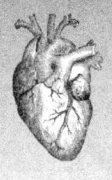

HOWIE REACHED THE BOTTOM RUNG AND HOPPED OFF THE SLOPE, feeling the pain pulse through his body with the impact of the ground. Cory followed him down, standing at the hilltop and taking in the chaos below. There was one thing Howie wanted to make sure got done before they left this hell behind them. He walked around the back of the slope, intentionally avoiding Todd's body in his peripheral. The thought of seeing his friend impaled by the tree was unbearable, and he couldn't bring himself to see it again. Once he got past the body, he found what he was looking for. On the ground in front of him, Jessica's decapitated head sat in a pile of leaves, staring off to the side. The look of her face, frozen in place with an expression of surprise, was one of the ugliest things Howie had ever seen. He took his bag and unzipped it; the bag now empty after he'd used all the supplies he packed. After a deep breath, he reached down and picked up her head by the ear. Green pus dripped from the opening in the neck, oozing down Howie's hand. He turned his head to the side and gagged, then dropped the head into his backpack. When he turned around, Cory was looking at him like he had a third eye in his forehead.

"What the actual fuck are you doing, Howie?"

"I'm making sure this is over. The occult expert in that video said they needed to be burned," Howie replied.

Shaking his head, Cory said "Well, how would you explain her rising up out of the fire like the damn T-1000 in *Terminator 2*? She didn't seem to mind the fire then," Cory said.

"I think whatever that demon was, it was just shedding Jessica's skin in the fire. Had she been in there any longer, her actual body would have burned away."

After thinking about it for a moment, Cory shrugged his shoulders and started to limp down the hill as he held his arm across his wounded chest. Howie followed, hoping he had a chance to toss the bag in the fire before the cops questioned him.

When they got to the bonfire, he was thankful that one of the cops or firefighters had already put a sheet over some of the victim's bodies, including Ryan's. He wasn't sure he could function if he saw Ryan burned to a crisp again. The fire had diminished to a simmer, but still burned strongly enough for what he intended to do. Howie tossed his backpack, watching it land dead center in the burning flames. The colors in the fabric melted away, and before long, his bag was a thing of the past. He kept his eyes locked on the spot, fear in the back of his head telling him to make sure she was gone for good.

"Howie? Cory?" a familiar voice asked from behind.

He turned around to see Bethany walking toward them with a smile on her face, happy to see them alive. She ran up to them, hugging Cory as tears rolled down her cheeks.

"Thank God, I really thought you guys were gone," she said.

Cory winced from the hug, the wounds on his chest causing intense pain. She backed off, realizing what she had just done.

"Oh no, I'm so sorry. Are you okay?"

Cory let out a half-hearted laugh before saying, "Well, I feel like a bus just ran over me, but seeing you helps ease the pain."

She smiled and kissed his cheek. "I went to the police station. Apparently, they'd been trying to radio Officer Miller all night but said he turned off his radio. Any idea why he would avoid having help come?"

Howie figured the less she knew, the better. At least for now. He locked eyes with Cory, and knew he agreed.

"Maybe it was some mix up, his radio could've been damaged or something during the riot," Howie said.

She seemed to accept the answer and walked with Cory toward the closest ambulance to get help. Cory got into the back of the ambulance with Bethany. As he walked away, Howie couldn't shake something he had just seen. At first glance, he assumed the reflection of the fire in the glass window had played tricks on him. In the dark space of the vehicle, Cory's eyes let off a faint orange glow.

The door slammed shut and the ambulance pulled out of the parking lot, driving off into the distance.

THE END

ACKNOWLEDGMENTS

There are so many thanks to be given out for my first novel. I will start by thanking my wife Danielle and my kids Will and Elizabeth. I tried as hard as possible to write when it would not impact family time, but let's face it, even when you are not writing, the story is in your headspace. It's impossible to turn the switch off. They have supported me through this crazy journey, and for that I am grateful. I would also like to thank a few people that have helped me with research for the book, as well as helping with the process from start to finish on self-publishing a novel. Joshua Marsella, who I met as a guest on my podcast, has been crucial. He helped introduce me to a cover artist, editor, even formatted this limited edition of the book. I have benefited from some of Joshua's early learning experiences that he was kind enough to share with me and we chat almost every day now. I also want to thank Nick White, who many may be familiar with from his show on A&E about the Bell Witch. He was also a guest on our show but has stayed in touch with me ever since. I pick his brain about witches, demons, curses, you name it. He has helped fill some holes that I would not have caught in the plot. If any occult experts read this book and find unrealistic things happening, just know that's on me, not Nick. I may have taken the liberty with some of the stuff he told me and tweaked it to fit the plot of my book. Joseph Sale is a magician as much as he is an editor. Joseph took my novel and polished it up so wonderfully, it would not have turned into the book it is without him. Matt Seff Barnes designed the incredible cover and was a delight to work with. I provided him with an idea I had, and he took that idea and made it far better than I could have ever imagined. Thank you to all the horror legends I looked up to over the years that helped pave the way for me and inspired me enough to chase this crazy dream. Stephen King got me into horror, authors like Brian Keene, Ronald Kelly, and so many more have been so kind to me along the way, allowing me to pick their brains, talk on our show, and do anything to help the next wave of horror authors trying to make a name for themselves. And lastly, but certainly not least, thank you dear reader for giving a new author a shot and picking up my book to read. I hope you enjoyed it, and I can promise I will only get better as I grow as a writer. Until next time...

November 6, 2022

ABOUT THE AUTHOR

John is a proud HWA member and lifelong horror fan who decided to chase his childhood dream of becoming a horror author. Growing up in New Hampshire, he discovered Stephen King much younger than most probably should have, reading IT before he reached high school—and knew from that moment on he wanted to write horror.

He co-founded Livid Comics in late 2020, co-creating and writing his debut comic titled Jol (pronounced Yule), a Christmas horror series for all ages. After publishing that, the itch to expand his writing was one he had to scratch.

Through Livid, he wrote his second comic due to be released this winter titled Dead Ball. John also co-launched a podcast called The Livid Comics Lair, where they talk with many of today's best horror authors, comic creators, and all things that go bump in the night like UFO and paranormal investigators.

His true passion was always to write horror novels, and in 2021 he started submitting short stories in hopes of getting noticed in the horror community and launching a career. He had his first story accepted in the summer of 2021 in the Books of Horror anthology, and an alternate version of the story in the Beach Bodies anthology from DarkLit Press.

Coming up, John has multiple stories to be released in the

prose and comic world in 2023. (Yes, there will be a sequel to The Cursed Among Us, likely in 2024, titled Consumed By Evil.)

Twitter: @jdurgin1084
Website: www.johndurginauthor.com
Youtube Channel: Livid Comics

UPCOMING WORKS

January 2023 - Inside The Devil's Nest, courtesy of D&T Publishing

Winter 2023 - Dead Ball Issue 2, courtesy of Livid Comics

Spring 2023 - Sleeping In The Fire, a collection of short stories

Late 2023 - Kosa: a novel

Printed in Great Britain
by Amazon